ESCAPE FROM
STALINGRAD

ESCAPE FROM STALINGRAD

ANDY MARINO

Scholastic Inc.

ISBN 978-1-338-85856-3

10 9 8 7 6 5 4 3 2 1   23 24 25 26 27

First edition, September 2023
Printed in the U.S.A.   40

Book design by Christopher Stengel

FOR LIAM

CHAPTER

AUGUST 1942

"Will you fight to defend the motherland?"

The commissar pauses to let his question sink in. His bright eyes sweep the faces of the crowd at the edge of the square beneath the towering copper statue of Vladimir Lenin. The founder of Soviet Russia points into the glorious future, and the shadow of his finger gently nudges Artem Romanovich Sokolov.

Artem steps aside so that the shadow falls to the pavement. At the same time, he turns the commissar's word over in his mind.

Motherland.

Rodina.

Artem has heard the word spoken aloud his entire twelve-year-old life, yet he's never really pondered its meaning. He glances up at the impassive face of his own mother—as carved and stonelike as the statue that looms above them all—and then out at the bone-white buildings that line the square. He scans the distant rooftops. A trio of white-winged birds alights upon a chimney top.

Cranes, Artem thinks, feeling for the sketch pad tucked into his shirt pocket. *Those migratory ones with the black necks . . .*

He racks his brain for the name of their species. It is rare to see them inside the city. With the name of the birds on the tip of his tongue, he watches them lift off from the chimney and glide south along the square. Their shadows flicker across the central fountain as they wheel away out of view. *Flying south a few months early.* Artem wonders if they, too, have gotten word of the Nazi invasion—the hundreds of thousands of German soldiers and Panzer tanks that have already overrun Rostov, a mere three hundred kilometers from Stalingrad.

"Yes, comrade commissar!" The reply comes in unison from each citizen's throat with triumphant force. Pulled from his thoughts, Artem's voice trails the crowd, too late. His older brother, Vasily, glares down at him—but Artem can see the amusement in the way his brother's eyebrow lifts. He can also see the little red mark on the underside of his brother's jaw where Vasily cut himself shaving. At seventeen and very fair-haired, Vasily barely needs to shave at all, but this morning he lathered up and dragged the razor across his skin before putting on his new Red Army uniform.

"I know you will," the commissar assures the crowd. "I can see the spirit of the revolution still burns in each and every one of you gathered here today."

Morning sun glints off the red star medallion on the front of the commissar's cap. Unlike some of the other political officers, this commissar does not strut around driving Party slogans like hammered railroad ties into the brains of the citizens of Stalingrad. This commissar does not even stand on a podium, though one has been wheeled into place for the morning's assembly. He does not pace like a military commander inspecting his ranks. He walks among his fellow citizens. He is a man of the people, like Comrade Stalin. He even slouches a bit. He takes off his cap, glances up at the relentless sun, scratches at his thick head of hair. He draws the attention of the crowd to a red banner that hangs like a lolling tongue from a balcony: a military council poster. Artem's sharp eyes take in the words.

WE SHALL NEVER SURRENDER THE CITY OF OUR BIRTH.

The commissar strides through the crowd as it gently parts to let him through. He flings an arm to gesture beyond the central fountain at a neat row of spruce trees pruned into oblong shapes.

"These trees were planted in 1925, on the day they changed the name of your glorious city from Tsaritsyn to Stalingrad to honor Comrade Stalin himself. He who so bravely defended the city during the revolution. These trees belong to you. They spring from the soil of your history. Will you let the Nazi tanks bulldoze them?"

"No, comrade commissar!" This time, Artem's voice rings out in time with the others'. Vasily places his hand on Artem's shoulder and gives it a squeeze.

The commissar moves through the crowd. He is not a tall man and he disappears into the throng. Artem stands on tiptoes. A moment later he spots the red star on the man's cap, bobbing lightly in the sea of his fellow citizens, all of them turned out in public squares across the city by order of the defense committee to receive their assignments. Artem loses sight of the red star again, just as the man's voice rises furiously.

"The Palace of Pioneers!" the commissar calls out. Artem feels a jolt of excitement at the mention of his favorite place in Stalingrad. He has spent countless hours in the building's laboratory, studying the natural sciences, dissecting owl pellets, and drawing the skeletons of rodents while his schoolmates practice piano, ballet, and chess. "Where your children hone the skills that will feed our Soviet culture for decades to come, and the talents to power our science academies to new heights! Will you let it become a boardinghouse for Nazi officers?"

"No, comrade commissar!"

A ripple of energy moves through the crowd as if blasted from the shadowy fingertip of Lenin himself.

The commissar's voice rings out louder and closer. "Will you let it become a place of light and learning and joy for the Nazi children of the Third Reich?"

"No, comrade commissar!"

The man in front of Artem abruptly steps to the side to reveal the commissar. Artem's eyes move up from the shadow at his feet to note the red stripes on the sleeves of the officer's sharply creased tunic, the shine of the brim of his cap, the glint in his eyes as he lowers his gaze to Artem. Vasily's hand gives him a subtle push. Artem does not dare take his attention away from the commissar, but at the same time, those cranes flash across his vision. Oh, to be able to fly away, to join the flock and soar out over the empty steppe, far from advancing Nazis and Red Army commissars and a city about to become a battleground.

What would happen if he voiced such thoughts to a man like the commissar? He would bring shame to his entire family, for one. Such thoughts are defeatist. Cowardly.

Treasonous.

The commissar drops to one knee. His head is at the same height as Artem's. The crowd forms a circle around them. Artem does his best not to squirm under the political officer's gaze.

"What is your name?" he asks with what sounds like genuine interest.

Vasily gives his shoulder another squeeze. Artem swallows.

"Artem Romanovich Sokolov."

"Artem Romanovich, what do you like best about our city?"

"The animals," he says without hesitation.

The commissar blinks. He clearly did not expect this answer, but he recovers quickly and gives Artem a gentle smile. "Which ones?"

"The sparrows and the cranes. The bullfrogs on the banks of the Volga. The stray dogs up on the Mamayev Kurgan." He pauses. "My cat, Misha."

"Misha," the commissar repeats.

A few of the men nearby start to chuckle. Artem feels, all at once, like a very small boy, a little snot-nosed kid thrust into a serious, grown-up situation.

Artem stands as straight as he can. "It's because I want to be a veterinarian," he explains to the commissar. A sense of how to speak to such men, which every Soviet citizen understands practically from birth, takes over. He adds a line the political officer would surely approve of. "I want to make sure the oxen and horses of our collective farms are healthy so they can work hard."

The commissar nods sharply. His bright eyes seem to sparkle. Artem notes that one of his eyes is blue, the other brown. Just behind him, he can sense a release of tension from Vasily and his mother. A breathing out.

The commissar rises to his feet and holds up a hand to silence the murmuring crowd.

"You see how the dreams of the state, the dreams of the Party, and the dreams of this boy, Artem Romanovich, are as one? They cannot be separated. This boy is Russia." He points at Artem, mirroring the statue at

Artem's back, whose long shadow creeps out over the crowd. The commissar raises his voice. "This boy is all of us." He shouts, "And we are the *motherland*!"

A ragged cheer sweeps the crowd—the high-pitched hooting and clapping of a football match joining with the *URRAH* of the infantry charge from soldiers like his brother.

Something stirs inside Artem—a similar feeling to when he's been observing a sparrow's nest for hours and the mother bird flies home with food for her babies. Exhilaration at the natural order of things playing out before his eyes. A process that's secret and also universal.

All across Russia, from the steppes to the streets of great cities, civilians and soldiers alike are called upon to repel the Nazi hordes piercing the heart of the Rodina.

Artem feels strong hands under his arms. Vasily lifts him up with one smooth motion so he can see the commissar bound to the front of the crowd. Now, at last, the man takes the podium.

"Will you fight for Artem Romanovich and the animals?" the commissar thunders. He grips the sides of the podium and leans forward, wide-eyed.

Cries of "Yes, comrade commissar!" mingle with long, unbroken shouts.

"Will you fight for your mothers, your fathers, your sons, your daughters"—the commissar is overtaken by the screaming crowd. His voice rises into hysteria—"your *babushkas* in their easy chairs?!"

Artem, held aloft by his brother, is carried even higher by the fierceness of the crowd's conviction. Even his mother is joining the chorus, her reedy voice unleashed upon the morning air. The commissar waves his arms, gesturing at the statue and beyond, out to the cold and choppy Volga river, north toward the massive labyrinth of factories and workers' huts.

Across the square, a stooped old man tosses bits of bread to the ducks that hang around the central fountain. Artem finds that it makes him angry. Who is this old man to go about his business as if the Nazis weren't practically at the gates of the city?

Suddenly, the commissar gestures for quiet. The crowd simmers down. The aftermath of their passion seems to hang in the air like mist.

The commissar continues in a more measured voice. "In his Order Number 227, Comrade Stalin has made things very plain. *Not one step back.*" He turns his head from side to side. His red star flashes. "Anyone who retreats—anyone who *speaks of retreat*—is a coward and a traitor. Cowards and traitors will be shot. It's as simple as that. There is no land for you beyond the Volga. Your land is here. To let it fall into Nazi hands is death. To run away from the battle is death!"

The commissar goes on about the grim fates awaiting panic-mongers and defeatists. The crowd falls silent. Each of them, Artem guesses, is trying to locate their courage like he is, as if it's something he can draw up from inside himself like water from a well. Still held high in his brother's strong arms, Artem spies a single crane, left behind, perched regally upon a balcony. A moment later it flies away to join its brothers and sisters somewhere in the safety of the endless, silent steppe.

CHAPTER

The woman from the district party committee leafs through the pages of a thick binder. The huge crowd has been funneled to booths set up along the edges of Lenin Square, divided by neighborhood. As they wait in line, Artem nods at the neighbors he recognizes from their corner of the central district, just south of the Mamayev Kurgan, the massive ancient hill that divides the northern industrial district, with its factory complexes like small towns, and the more residential southern districts.

"Sokolov," she says, stabbing a fingertip into a block of text in the middle of a page.

She looks up from the binder and regards Artem's mother, Vasily, and Artem in turn. Her pursed lips are a thin line. Her sharp nose and cheekbones seem to stretch her skin in angles that remind Artem of the rodent-like face of the vesper bat, which he dissected at the Palace of

Pioneers. She glances back down at the page where her finger is still planted.

"Roman Andreyovich Sokolov," she reads, "deceased."

At this mention of the father he never knew, Artem's eyes shift to his mother. Her face remains impassive.

"Correct," she says.

The district committee woman makes a tiny check mark in black ink.

"Anna Olegovna Sokolov."

"Present," Artem's mother says. Another check mark goes in the book.

"Vasily Romanovich Sokolov."

"Present." Check.

"Artem Romanovich Sokolov."

"Present." Check.

The district committee woman closes the binder, slides it to the side of the rickety metal desk, and opens a second, even thicker, binder. She leafs through page after page, muttering softly to herself. Artem's attention wanders to a nearby spruce tree, where a pair of squirrels chase each other up the trunk. Squirrels are of the family Sciuridae, which is easy for Artem to remember because they like to *scurry*. One squirrel with a bushier tail races out to the end of a branch and stops on a dime.

"The three of you are assigned to the building of earth walls to protect our petroleum storage tanks," the committee woman says, reading from a page of crowded text. She looks up. "Beginning tomorrow morning at six, you will report to the district party headquarters. You will be issued tools and materials. You will be issued badges." She flips through a folder and slides a sheet of paper across the desk. "This is form 652-C. You must bring it to the party headquarters or you will not be issued your badges. Badges must be displayed at all times. Failure to display your badges will result in punishment."

Artem's mother picks up the paper. "*Two* of us have to report, you mean."

The woman stares back blankly. Then she shifts her eyes to the long line of citizens behind them. "*Three* of you, I said."

"So you did, but my elder son, Vasily"—she nudges him with her elbow—"is in the Red Army."

"I'm shipping out to the front this afternoon," Vasily explains. "Fifty-First Guards Rifle Division. I won't be here tomorrow morning."

"All *three* of you must report to the party headquarters at six to receive your city defense assignments," the woman says, slightly irritated, as if these Sokolovs are simply too stupid to understand. "Anyone who fails to show up will be arrested."

Vasily steps forward and places his hands on the desk. "And if I fail to show up to my army unit, I will be executed for cowardice."

The woman shrugs. "Form 652-C orders the issuance of *three* city defense badges for the Sokolovs. Are you saying that the committee members who prepared this form are lying?"

"I am saying," Vasily says slowly, "that perhaps they are mistaken." He places a hand on his chest. "I am wearing the uniform of a Red Army private. I have been called to the front. I will be with my unit in the morning, not the party headquarters, so the committee will just have to adjust their badge count."

The woman takes a deep breath and lets it out, as if her patience is being severely tested. As if she blames Vasily for the mix-up. "The district committee will be held responsible for any unclaimed badges."

What this woman means, Artem thinks, is that *she* will be held responsible if exactly three Sokolovs do not show up at district party headquarters in the morning.

Vasily throws up his hands and glances around for help. Their neighbors from the central district look away, suddenly interested in the cobblestones of the square or the banner reminding everyone that *we shall never surrender the city of our birth.*

"If one member of a family does not claim his badge," the woman continues, "things could be very difficult for the other members of such a family."

Meaning, Artem figures, any trouble I get in with my superiors, *you* will take the blame. He glances out across the square, but the commissar is nowhere in sight. It occurs to him that the commissar and the district committee leader are like members of the same genus, but a different species. Like the brown bear and the polar bear—*Ursus arctos* and *Ursus maritimus.* Related, of course, but so very different. Both Communist Party functionaries, both tasked with the defense of the city, but with vastly different missions here today. How strange it is that the commissar could inspire such patriotic fervor, only to have it crushed by paperwork a moment later. Artem wishes he knew what to say to help his brother, but the woman makes him nervous. And he can feel the impatience seething from the line behind him, though he knows that no one will dare complain out loud.

If there's one thing his fellow Russians are used to, it's silently waiting in line.

His mother leans toward the woman. "Listen to me." She thrusts a finger into the air. "The skies will be black with German bombers any day now. Do you think this paperwork mix-up will still be an issue then, or will we all have bigger problems to deal with? *Comrade.*"

Vasily takes his mother by the arm and tries to pull her back. His mother does not move, as if her folded arms are made of steel. The committee leader does not flinch, simply glares back silently at Anna

Olegovna. Her hair is pulled back into a tight bun that seems to stretch her skin taut across those bat-like cheeks.

Vasily says something softly to their mother, something Artem cannot hear. Anna Olegovna seems to sag a little. The steel flows from her body and she allows herself to be pulled back. Artem has seen this play out a thousand times before. According to Vasily, she has been this way ever since the Party accused her husband—Artem's father—of disloyalty and sent him to die in the Siberian labor camps. Vasily had been five years old. Artem, seven months. Now, twelve years later, Vasily always knows what to say to their mother, like one of those old horse whisperers calming an unruly Arabian.

Suddenly, his brother's upcoming absence yawns before him. An unfillable void in his life, for Vasily is both kind and strong—the boy who taught him to kick a football, and climb trees on the Mamayev Kurgan, and run laughing through the Tsaritsa Gorge. But now it's a matter of what he *hasn't* been able to teach Artem. Vasily's soft touch with their mother, his way of getting through to her to defuse a dangerous situation with a Party functionary. If not for Vasily, Anna Olegovna would likely have been sent to a labor camp herself.

"We are sorry to be taking up so much of your time on such an important day, comrade," Vasily says. "But surely you can see that we are in an impossible situation through no fault of our own. We are not shirkers. I am headed for the front, and my mother and brother are reporting to city defense." He smiles. "Perhaps you can make a small edit to the form, so we are only responsible for claiming two badges? Then we can all do our part for the motherland without fear of a misunderstanding."

"If I can edit the form," she explains, "then *anyone* could simply edit their forms with the stroke of a pen. Then who's to say what's authorized and what is not?" She shakes her head. "It's out of the question. A new form must be generated."

Artem senses the nervous aggression of his mother's energy, like a lynx about to pounce on prey. Just beyond the table, the two squirrels scamper down the spruce trunk and bound across the cracked pavement of the square. A husky on a leash tries to bound after them, nearly yanking its owner off his feet. Artem's always wanted a husky, but Misha would be terrified.

"All right," Vasily says. "A new form, then."

The woman sighs. "I'm warning you, they won't be happy about it."

"Who?"

She points to a large white tent in front of the central fountain. Its flaps are pinned open, and on the inside of each flap is a red star. Artem tries to see inside, but yet another line of people blocks his view. The squirrels, spooked by the husky, caper around the fountain's rim.

"Take this to them," the woman says, indicating form 652-C.

Artem's mother snatches it from the table and stalks off to join the line snaking out of the white tent. Artem follows.

The shadow of Lenin's hand shrinks back toward the monument as the sun climbs higher in the sky.

CHAPTER

Halfway to the white tent, Artem's brother stops him with a hand on his shoulder. Artem looks up. He is tall for his age, and Vasily is short and stocky like their mother, so he only has to lift his head slightly to meet his brother's eyes. The shaving cut is a tiny red dot now, already crusted over. Artem wonders if soldiers can shave at the front. Do they even have warm water?

He realizes, all at once, that he has no idea what his brother's life is going to be like as a front-line soldier, one of the *frontoviki*. Everything happened so fast—one day Stalingrad was so far removed from the war engulfing all of Europe that it might as well have been on a different planet, and the next day the Germans were practically at the gates of the city. Everyone was stunned by the speed of the German advance. Panzer tanks lurching through Kiev, racing like leopards across the barren steppe, all the way to the oil fields of the Caucasus and the edge of

Stalingrad itself. Operation Blue, the Germans call this dagger stabbing into the heart of the Rodina. Artem finds this name odd—blue is a peaceful color, the color of sea and sky. He imagines war to be orange and red, shades of fire and blood.

"Artem," Vasily says. "I need to talk to you." Artem catches a blur of movement out of the corner of his eye. A large bird the color of sunset over the Volga lifts off from a treetop and spreads its wings.

"A kestrel!" Artem exclaims. "That makes two birds that shouldn't be this far into the city itself, and definitely not hanging out in Lenin Square! I saw these cranes earlier"—he snaps his fingers—"demoiselles, that's what they're called. Do you think they're flying away from the Germans, and that's why they've come all the way here?"

His brother grips him by the arms. "I think you need to quit watching birds, and feeding stray dogs, and sketching squirrels, and following rats into their holes."

"I don't follow rats." Artem pauses. "That doesn't even make sense. How could I fit—"

"Artem!" There is pained urgency in his brother's voice. He glances over his shoulder. Their mother has taken her place in line, arms folded, form 652-C clenched in her fist. Vasily turns back to Artem. "What I mean is, there is no more time for hobbies. I know it's not fair, but it's the way things are. Starting now. You have exactly two jobs: keeping yourself alive and looking after our mother. You must devote yourself to these things."

Artem feels a sort of hurt well up. His brother knows how serious he is about natural science and becoming a veterinarian. To call his pursuit a "hobby" makes him sound like a stupid little kid chasing butterflies. And besides—

"The commissar said we're all fighting for the animals, too," Artem says.

"Forget what the commissar said!" Vasily leans close to lower his voice. He glances around to make sure no one is within earshot. "Yes, we all must do our part for the motherland, that's not in doubt. But make no mistake, Artem, hard times are coming. Impossible times, maybe. And if it gets really bad, you're going to have to look after yourself and Mom—and that's it. Caring about animals is a great thing, Artem. It comes from a part of you that's innocent and good. But in the days to come, this city will be no place for the innocent or the good."

Artem tries to imagine the version of Stalingrad his brother is talking about. He thinks of his mother's remark about the sky, black with German planes. Both Vasily and his mother seem to be indulging in what the political officers call "defeatism"—the idea that it is a foregone conclusion that the Germans will win the battles at the gates and out on the steppe, and continue their advance to occupy the city. In school, Artem has learned that this kind of attitude is treasonous.

"But," Artem says, "you'll stop the Germans. The Red Army will—"

Vasily's voice is a whisper. "The Red Army will fight. And maybe we will beat them back." Artem blinks. *Maybe?* His brother doesn't sound very sure of himself. He thinks of the commissar's words, of Stalin's decree: *Cowards and traitors will be shot!* "Listen to me. I am telling you some very grown-up things, but you must listen and understand. And you must never repeat any of this, to anyone, not even in private. The first chance you get, whether it's tomorrow or next month, you take our mother and you cross the Volga. Go east. Don't stop until you reach the Ural Mountains."

"But," Artem says, keeping his own voice as low as his brother's, "Comrade Stalin said *not one step back*." He feels like he's being tossed about by a strange and unpredictable current. First the commissar had him ready to kill German soldiers with his bare hands. Then the woman from the district committee had dragged him back down to earth. And now his brother is telling him to escape at the first chance he gets from the city he just swore to defend.

The city that swirls around him now in a riot of movement and life. The beautiful old buildings lining the square, the perfectly pruned spruce trees, the burbling fountain, the chatter of sparrows . . .

Artem's gaze settles on the red banner unfurled from the balcony. He reads it aloud. "We shall never surrender the city of our birth." The words sound good on his tongue. There is a flavor to them, bold like *solyanka* soup.

Vasily sighs. He closes his eyes and drifts away for a moment, into his own head. When he opens his eyes again, they are hard and mean and sad.

"Comrade Stalin sent our father to the labor camps to die, Artem. For no reason. I know this might be hard to understand, but there is a difference between fighting to defend the motherland and fighting for Stalin and the Party. The motherland is worth defending. The motherland is home, and home is *you*. Keeping you safe is worth dying for. And I am in the Red Army—I accept my death as the price of this service. But as for Comrade Stalin's decree that *every citizen must die, too*?" Vasily spits on the ground. "You don't owe him that. If I am to die, I would rather die knowing that you and Mom are safe, that you have a long and full life ahead of you." He smiles thinly. "You and your animals."

"You're not going to die, Vasily," Artem says, but the words come out feeble and hollow. He has known death in many forms. Before Misha there had been Nadya, his tabby that had grown sickly and weak before his eyes. He has dissected mice and birds and even a pig at the Palace of Pioneers, studied their internal organs up close. And there had been an aunt, his mother's sister, who lived in one of the workers' settlements in the northern factory districts, who'd suffered from a heart condition . . .

So he has known death, and he is certain death is not something that fits Vasily. It is as if his brother were to try on the velvet cloak of some old Tsarist royal—so ill-fitting and out of place as to be absurd. Death is part of nature and it comes for sick pets and even old aunts and fathers you never knew—not your smart, strong, brave older brother.

The reality of this afternoon rushes at him like a mad herd of antelopes. There is nowhere for him to hide: It's happening, right now. His brother is leaving. And instead of sitting idly by and enduring whatever comes his way, Artem is going to have to step into Vasily's shoes.

There is no one else.

"Promise me, Artem. Whatever happens. You and Mom will get out, and live, and be happy far from here."

Artem's mind churns. *Across the Volga. East.* How far are the Ural Mountains? He's never been more than twenty kilometers from Stalingrad.

The commissar's voice echoes in his mind. *Not one step back.*

Artem swallows. "I promise."

Vasily stares into his eyes, unblinking, for what feels like a full minute. Then he gives him a firm nod and lets go of his arms. He straightens up and adjusts his army cap. Both brothers glance around the square, but Artem is sure no one overheard. Everyone is intent on lining up, finding their district committee booths, receiving their defense assignments.

Vasily stands as still as the great statue across the square. Artem tries to think of something to say. At the same time he forces down a horrible thought: *Better make it good, in case it's the last thing you ever say to him . . .*

He reaches into his pocket and retrieves his miniature sketchbook. He rips off a page at random. It's a drawing of a fuzzy, thick-bodied rodent he spotted on the banks of the river last month. He hands it to Vasily, who regards it curiously.

"It's a water vole."

"Thank you, Artem." Vasily folds it up and slides it neatly into the breast pocket of his uniform. "I'll call him Mitya."

Artem tries to laugh but makes a halting little sobbing noise instead. He flips through his sketchbook intently so his brother won't see his tears.

"Would you rather have an otter?"

"I'm already pretty attached to Mitya. That wouldn't be fair to him."

This time Artem manages to laugh. He pockets the sketchbook as his brother wraps him up in a hug. Then his brother holds him at arm's length to meet his eyes once more.

"Take care, Artem."

With that, Vasily turns away and melts into the crowd.

CHAPTER

Artem smears dirt on his forehead with the back of his hand. He jabs his rusted metal shovel into the mound at his feet and catches his breath.

"There should be a name for mud that's made with sweat instead of water," he says. He flicks his wrist. Gobs of wet earth go flying.

The girl watches him absently. She holds her shovel across her body, like a rifle, and waits for him to resume work. Artem and this girl were assigned as partners by the defense committee more than a week ago now, and in that span of twelve-hour days of moving dirt together, he still hasn't learned her name.

"It's hot!" he says, shielding his eyes and glaring up at the relentless summer sun. August in Stalingrad is a far cry from the brutal, endless winters the motherland is famous for. Artem is drenched in sweat. He finds that he actually feels bad for the political officers and Party functionaries overseeing the work in their suits and uniforms. He watches a portly commissar tilt back a canteen till the water runs down the front of his tunic. A tunic the color of a muskrat.

"At least we get to wear shorts," he says to the girl. She is dressed in a sort of uniform, too. It's kind of like a *Komsomol*—Communist youth group—outfit, with its dark blue skirt and white shirt. But it lacks the telltale red kerchief. She hasn't volunteered any information about it, and Artem has learned that it's pointless to ask. She doesn't respond. Artem watches her gaze off at the row of petroleum tanks that line the riverbank.

Even after a week of working in their shadow, the great fuel tanks are still a marvel. Silver cylinders the size of apartment buildings, each one topped with what looks like a giant metal cone-shaped hat. Artem imagines the millions of gallons of pungent fuel sloshing around inside each tank, flowing out to power the Red Army's trucks and tanks and troop carriers and fighter planes.

What is even more incredible to Artem is that this barren stretch of land, which houses these massive structures, is still part of the city itself, inside the boundaries of Stalingrad. Yet he has never even been to this district before. There are so many places within the city of his birth that he has never seen. He remembers his mother telling him, on their way to the northern district to pay a final visit to her dying sister, that the city once known as Tsaritsyn stretches for forty kilometers along the Volga.

Lost in the great shadows of the fuel tanks, surrounded by thousands of his fellow citizens piling up dirt to secure the walls, Artem feels a complicated surge of hope. After all, how many hundreds of thousands of Germans would it take to subdue such a vast city? How big is the army Hitler has sent this far east? Not big enough for such a monumental task, surely . . .

"Artem!" His mother calls out as she moves past him. "Quit daydreaming!" She and her partner, a younger woman with a perpetually gloomy look that clashes with her bright red hair, carry a stretcher piled high with dirt. "Be more like Yuna!" The two women bear their load over to the earth wall steadily growing around the base of the nearest fuel tank. Together, they sidle up the slope of the wall and tilt their dirt onto the top of the pile.

Astonished, Artem turns to see his partner shoveling great clods of dirt onto their own stretcher. "Yuna?" he says. "How does my mother know your name, but I don't?"

The girl shrugs. With great fury, she attacks the earth with her shovel.

"Oh!" It dawns on Artem all at once. "Your mother and my mother must be friends. Do you live in our neighborhood? I've never seen you around." He waits for an answer. Yuna shovels dirt. "What school do you go to?"

She dumps another pile on the stretcher, then tosses her shovel aside and grips the handles. She brushes wet strands of hair out of her face and looks at him expectantly.

Artem catches a squirmy movement atop the dirt and leans in for a closer look. "That's a fat worm!" He looks at Yuna. "Did you know worms breathe through their skin? It's true!"

The girl puts her hands on her hips.

"Okay, okay," Artem says, grabbing the handles at his end of the stretcher. "Not interested in worms."

The stretcher feels like it weighs a hundred kilograms. Artem thinks of Red Army medics carrying the wounded. He tries, once again, to imagine the life of a frontoviki, pretends he's bearing this heavy load under enemy fire. Bullets whizzing past his ears, shrapnel whistling past his legs. For her part, Yuna seems to manage the heavy weight easily. He composes his face so the strain doesn't show, but he knows his skin is as red as a bowl of borscht. Together they carry their dirt over to the growing wall surrounding the nearest silver tank. With a practiced motion, they swing the stretcher and dump it on the pile.

Artem gazes up at the rim of the fuel tank, a gleaming silver arc set off against the blue sky.

"How long do you think it's going to take us to build the wall that high?" Then he frowns, thinking. "Are we even supposed to build it that high? What's the goal here?"

"To work until they tell us to stop," a man says, coming up next to him to dump his own stretcher. "Same as always."

Yuna is already on her way back to their shovels, sticking out of the ground like crooked grave markers. Dirt clings to her ankles and calves. Across the once-flat expanse now pocked with holes and mounds, Artem spots his mother and her downcast partner filling their stretcher with dirt. They are methodical—a strong, silent machine. His mother's kerchief is damp with sweat. He wonders if the frontoviki have to dig their own trenches. Maybe the trenches are already there? He surveys the massive dirt field and thinks of the old ditches from the civil war that still slice like dry rivers through parts of the city, overgrown with grass. In one, they actually found a huge family of stoats living there like they owned the place.

He closes his eyes. There is a cloud-thought coming on. He has named them cloud-thoughts because they are big and puffy and oddly shaped, and they hang in his head like a storm cloud ready to burst—but they never quite rain, so the point of the thought is always out of reach. This particular cloud-thought is something about the strangeness of people and the holes they dig, like Artem and a thousand others are doing right now. Holes that serve a purpose for a while, until the people who fought the war are all dead and the grass grows back over the holes and the animals move back in like nothing ever happened.

He surveys the landscape and tries to make his cloud-thought rain, but it only gets bigger and bigger in his mind, the meaning drifting away in wisps he can never quite grasp. Imagining the stoats and rabbits and mice that will one day live in the holes he and Yuna have dug, Artem picks up the empty stretcher and jogs to catch up with his partner.

"Sorry!" he says, laying the stretcher flat next to a fresh patch of earth. "I was just . . . thinking about something."

Yuna folds her arms, regards him with an inscrutable look, then swipes the back of her hand across her cheek. All it does is smear the dirt into the sweat-mud mix. Artem is about to point this out but keeps his mouth shut. Yuna just shakes her head and picks up her shovel. Artem grabs his—the metal handle aggravates the blisters that have formed, popped, and formed again on his palms—when a loud voice crackles out into the air from the loudspeakers posted on nearby lampposts.

"Attention, comrades!"

A low groan sweeps through the workers. They have heard this false alarm a million times. Nothing ever happens.

"An air-raid warning has been sounded in the city!"

Yuna continues to dig. Artem's eyes search the sky.

"Attention, comrades!" The tireless voice is on a never-ending loop.

The sun glints off a bright bird cruising in from the west, heading across the city toward the river. Artem shields his eyes. Another crane, with plumage so oily that it reflects the light. The voice on the loudspeaker recedes to the back of his mind. The advancing bird shimmers in the summer sun, then sharpens abruptly. Its shape and purpose become clear.

Artem thrusts out an arm, points to what is most certainly an airplane.

"Bomber!" he shouts.

In a matter of seconds the plane is close enough for Artem to make out the white and black crosses of the Luftwaffe—the German air force—on the underside of its wings.

And the Nazi swastika on its tail.

He scans the empty sky for any sign of Red Army fighters screaming in to intercept the bomber. But there is nothing—not even the dark cloudburst explosions of antiaircraft fire from the batteries across the river. No surprise there—he has heard rumors that there are not enough shells for the massive guns, and not enough trained soldiers to operate them. In fact, some kids from his class, girls from the Komsomol, have been recruited to be antiaircraft gunners. His mind, churning rapidly, settles on an image of quiet little Yevgenia Pavlova closing one eye, aiming down the barrel of a massive gun, lining up the Nazi plane in her crosshairs—

"Artem, get down!"

Just before he tears himself away from the sight of the airplane, its glass-and-steel nose comes into view, a transparent bubble spitting out a pair of guns.

He turns to see his mother running toward him, kicking up dirt, a giant fuel tank rising behind her. Her checked kerchief trails her head like comet's tail, then goes flying off and flutters away behind her.

All around him, his fellow citizens are leaping down into holes, curling up and covering their heads like they've all been taught by the political officers.

Duck and cover. Right.

He crouches down, places a hand on the rim of the hole he and Yuna have been gradually digging, and jumps into it like a frontoviki sheltering in his trench.

A sudden change comes over the workers. A kind of sweaty, expectant silence. The only voice is the sprightly announcer crackling from the loudspeaker.

"Attention, comrades!"

Artem looks up in time to see the German plane lay a long silver egg from its belly. The bomb is a surprisingly floaty thing, hanging in the air for much longer than Artem would have thought. The plane's engine *brraaaapppps* into his head and guts as it passes just north of his position and banks to follow the river, as if taunting the big flak guns on the east bank—which *still have not fired*.

Meanwhile the bomb is plastered to the blue sky. His mother is still too far away, calling his name. Artem's gaze sweeps along the rim of the hole, across Yuna's muddy ankles—

"Yuna, down here!" he calls out.

The girl is frozen upright, staring at the sky, transfixed. The bomb falls slowly at first, some lazy meandering thing that might even be friendly, instead of a weapon pointed at the heart of Russia. Artem grabs Yuna's leg. As if it suddenly wakes from its sleep, the bomb's nose tilts downward and it plunges at great speed toward the earth. He tugs at Yuna's leg but she does not move. The bomb falls faster. He wraps both hands around the girl's ankles and pulls as hard as he can. Her body pitches forward and he drags her into the hole.

They go down in a tangled heap. He thinks she is screaming at him. Then he realizes she's just screaming. A split second later she's drowned out by a deafening blast that seems to originate in the pit of his stomach and deep within the earth at the same time. Artem screams, too, clamping his hands over his ears, squeezing his eyes shut, planting himself facedown in the dirt. Yuna's arm is hinged around the crook in his elbow, her knee digging into his back. Chunks of earth rain down on them. If steel and razor-sharp shrapnel is to follow, there is nothing they can do.

Ducking and covering, he realizes, is useless. It's silly to think that placing your hands over your head can offer any protection against a Nazi bomb dropped from the sky.

Something big thuds into their hole. Artem braces himself for another explosion. He wonders what it will feel like. If it will feel like anything at all.

"Artem!" His mother's voice. Cautiously, he raises his head and opens one eye.

Anna Olegovna is sitting with her back against the side of the hole, hugging her knees to her chest. Her straw-colored hair is plastered to her head, and her wide eyes take in the hopeless tangle of Artem and Yuna.

Gently yet firmly, she crawls over and untangles them—pulling free an arm, then a leg. The three of them huddle together at the bottom of the hole. Artem's limbs are stiff and sore, and he realizes he's been tensing all his muscles. He tries to relax. Blood rushes in his ringing ears. The smell of churned-up earth hangs in the air. His mother brushes dirt from their shoulders and faces and the tops of their heads. She pauses with her rough hand on Artem's cheek and looks him in the eyes.

"We're all right, Artem. The bomb hit north of us," she says. "Closer to the riverbank."

She sounds curiously far away. Artem realizes that the disembodied voice of the air-raid warning is still looping across the field. *Attention, comrades!* The voice mingles with echoes of his mother's words. *Bomb. North. Riverbank.*

We're all right.

He blinks. Next to him, Yuna's clenching her body like a fist. Her eyes are squeezed shut and her hands are clamped over her ears. She is muttering to herself.

Anna Olegovna takes her by the wrists and lowers her arms. Yuna's eyes stay closed.

"Yuna," she says. "It's over. The bomber is gone."

The girl's eyelids tremble.

"It didn't hit us," Artem says. Even his own voice sounds hollow, as if he's speaking into a bucket. "I mean, obviously." He holds out his arms, presents them for inspection. Filthy but intact.

His mother gives him a look advising him to shut up.

The air-raid warning goes silent. In its place, a siren shrieks. Artem peeks over the rim of the hole. At least half a kilometer north, through a haze of grit and smoke, he can see a red cross painted on the side of a boxy green ambulance. The vehicle jounces along the ragged earth toward little scraps of scattered colors. He thinks he catches sight of a bright red Komsomol kerchief. A man comes running, waving his hands above his hand, flagging down the ambulance. A field nurse follows with a limp bundle in her arms. Artem turns away.

"Comrades!" A new voice bursts from the lamppost speakers. "The danger has passed. Return to work!"

Anna Olegovna mutters a curse. Using her sleeve, she wipes more dirt from Artem's face. Then she turns to Yuna.

"You're coming home with us tonight."

It isn't an invitation. It's an order. With that, she climbs up out of the hole to rejoin her partner.

Artem flicks a small, shiny beetle from Yuna's shoulder. She flinches.

“That little guy’s called *Sphaerius*,” he says. There’s a moment of silence. “So anyway, do you like *shchi*? We’re probably having shchi for dinner. We have it a lot. Like everybody, I guess.”

Artem tries to smile. Yuna sits silently, staring into the dirt, watching the beetle crawl away.

CHAPTER

The framed photograph of Artem's father presides over the cramped kitchen. It hangs above the stove, protected from grease and other spatters by a thin sheet of glass that his mother cleans every morning. In the photograph, his father wears a spotless white lab coat. Uncapped pens crowd the ink-stained pocket. An electron microscope is slightly out of focus on the table behind him. His face is smooth and unlined but there is a crinkly mischief in his smile. His warm, penetrating eyes are the prototypes for Vasily's, and the wild sweep of dark hair that curls like a tidal wave down over the side of his forehead is just like Artem's.

Artem watches Yuna study the picture as she waits for her shchi—cabbage soup—to cool. His mother pours them weak tea from the samovar. Artem winces as he lifts his glass. The blisters on his hands are raw and tender, and dirt is caked under his fingernails. He washed up as best he could before dinner, but a full day of digging in the sun has a way of seeping into his pores so that he always feels slightly unclean, even after a bath. His mother offers Yuna a piece of black bread, and she devours it like a ravenous chipmunk without taking her eyes off the photograph.

"My husband," Anna Olegovna says to Yuna as she sets a piece of bread in front of Artem. "Roman Andreyovich was a biology professor at the state university."

Artem nibbles his bread. With food rationed and supplies diverted to the front, he has taken to eating slowly to make their meager dinners last longer. He watches Yuna glance curiously around the tiny kitchen. He follows her gaze as it flows along the tiny stove top where the big pot of soup sits steaming alongside the samovar; the counter jammed with glasses, plates, and mugs; the ladles, spatulas, and pans hanging from hooks on the wall; the washboard propped in the corner beneath an apron and a pair of Artem's trousers drying on a line. He follows her train of thought, too: *Surely the family of a university professor ought to be living in a nicer flat in a nicer neighborhood than the slums just south of Mamayev Kurgan . . .*

Artem watches Yuna's eyes go to the tiny window. From their ground-floor flat, all that's visible is the drab gray brick of the identical apartment block across the street. It's a far cry from the gorgeous old buildings that rise proudly over Lenin Square with their ornate balconies festooned with red banners. Architecture that makes Artem think of the great capitals of the West—Paris, London, Vienna. His street just makes him think of cabbage soup and noises through thin walls.

"We used to have a *dacha*!" he blurts out. He's not sure why—he's not exactly *ashamed* of where he lives. And it's not like he ever got to see their little cottage in the woods outside the city that his father's position once afforded him. He's only ever heard about it from Vasily.

Yuna's eyes go wide. "I've never been to a dacha before."

Artem grins. "She speaks! The girl has a voice after all!"

"Yes," his mother says. "Of course she does. We have had many conversations, Yuna and I."

Artem frowns. "Really? When?" He looks at Yuna, then his mother. "About what?"

"Your habit of daydreaming when you're supposed to be working, for one," his mother says.

"It's not *daydreaming* when I'm taking mental notes on all the new animals I'm seeing," Artem says. "Did you know that the field over by the fuel tanks is home to a species of marsh frogs that you can only find . . ."

He trails off. An echo of Vasily's voice resounds in his head.

There is no more time for hobbies.

"Forget it," Artem says. He sips his tea, then drops the remainder of his bread into his soup, just like Vasily always used to do. He turns to Yuna. "So you can speak, you just don't feel like talking to me? Even though we're out there all day, every day, together?"

Yuna's eyes meet his mother's.

Anna Olegovna sighs. "Artem, I told her not to say anything to you. I know how easily distracted you are. I thought it better that you learn to stay focused on your work."

Artem pokes at the bread chunk with his spoon until it begins to break apart in the steaming broth. "Oh," he says.

First Vasily, now his mother. He feels like some kind of freak, what they call an *aberration* in the natural sciences. An animal who acts against the behaviors and instincts of his species. A child who chases animals when everyone else does the work to safeguard the motherland.

He feels like what the Party calls a parasite. The opposite of a worker. A drain on society.

He glances up at the photograph of his father, Roman Andreyovich Sokolov. He has the eerie feeling that his father would understand his obsessions. Encourage them, even with the Germans bearing down on the city. It's silly, of course—Artem never knew the man.

"I'm sorry," Yuna says softly. She places her hand above her bowl, palm down.

"It's okay," Artem says. "What are you doing?"

"The steam feels good on my blisters." She has a nice voice, Artem decides.

"Artem, listen to me," his mother says. "We are lucky to be assigned to the petroleum tanks."

He laughs. "Lucky?"

She is deadly serious. "Sofia Anatolyovna's two boys were caught napping in one of the holes by the southernmost tank, and the commissar had them sent to the front."

"Grigory and Vlad?" Artem pictures the twins, a few grades ahead of him. "They're only fourteen."

"They are to be trained as artillery spotters," his mother says. "Stationed atop buildings and hills to direct fire. Which means the Germans will target them." She shakes her head. "Suicide missions." Her eyes bore into Artem's. "*That* is why I begged Yuna not to talk to you. So some commissar doesn't catch you gabbing and send you off to a dangerous place."

Artem thinks of this afternoon's bombing raid. "Aren't we already in a dangerous place?"

It seems unreal to him, and he has to use a good bit of energy to remind himself that it actually happened. He wishes he could dismiss it as a nightmare to be shoved down and forgotten. But fragmented images are burned into his memory. The field nurse carrying what looked like a bundle of rags . . .

"Eat your soup," his mother says.

Artem digs into his bowl of potatoes, tomatoes, and cabbage. It's not as rich and hearty as his mother's shchi in peacetime, with its hard-to-get ingredients like butter and cream. But it's still not bad, even after eating it several times a week.

Next to him, Yuna plants her elbows on the table and attacks her soup. "This is wonderful," she says through mouthfuls of potato. Before Artem is halfway done, Yuna plunks her spoon down in her empty bowl.

"Doesn't your mother feed you?" Artem says. He means it as a lighthearted joke, but it comes out sounding irritable and mean.

"Artem!" his mother says sharply. "That is an extremely rude question." She softens her voice for Yuna. "Don't answer him. My son spends so much time with his animals, occasionally he forgets how to be human."

"It's okay," Yuna says. She turns to Artem. "I don't have a mother."

Artem freezes with his spoon halfway to his mouth. He feels his face begin to get hot. "Oh."

"Or a father," Yuna says.

Now he knows why she's wearing a uniform that's almost—but not quite—Komsomol. She lives at a *detsky dom*. A children's home. An orphanage.

He reaches for something to say, misses, and stays quiet. Nothing sounds quite right. A wave of exhaustion hits him all at once. He realizes now that it has been building since the bomb strike, waiting for his shock and adrenaline to subside before it swamps him. He puts down his spoon and rubs his eyes. It all seems so unreal. Just last month, his older brother walked him to school, the Germans were impossibly far away, and Stalingrad bustled along as it always had. Now his days are filled with commissars and shovels and dirt and bombs and now an orphan girl at their table.

Just as it all seems like too much, there's a soft nuzzle against his ankle.

"Cat attack!" he exclaims, grateful for the interruption. He slides his chair back, lifts the cat, and places him in his lap.

"This is Misha," he says to Yuna. Misha is a short-haired black-and-white cat, spotted like a cow, with a patch like a little half mustache just below his nose. He regards Yuna with mild suspicion. Artem can feel Misha's claws flexing, not exactly digging into his thighs but warning him that it's a possibility. "He was born in an alley. I found him when he was a kitten."

"The master of the house," Anna Olegovna says, getting up for more tea.

Cautiously, Yuna holds out a dirty hand to pet the cat.

"Start with his head," Artem says. "That's how you gain his trust."

She moves her fingertips along the top of his head, then gives him little scratches behind his ears. Misha begins to purr. Artem can feel the cat relax his claws.

"Here," Artem says when Misha has gone fully calm. He lifts the cat and places him in Yuna's lap. Misha nudges the back of her hand with his nose until she resumes petting his head. She looks at Artem with a funny expression on her face. It is so unfamiliar, it takes him a moment to realize that Yuna is smiling.

CHAPTER

The next morning, commotion in the living room pulls Artem from a dream of swimming in the Volga. He rises out of the water toward his brother and wakes to a bright, sunny day. It is August 23. A Sunday.

Normally, it would be his one day off from school. He would head to the Palace of Pioneers, visit Dr. Petrakov in her lab, joke about how she never left the place, not even to eat or sleep. She would show him the pig's eye or the sparrow heart, neatly bisected on the tray by her microscope. But these aren't normal times, and there is no rest for those working on the city's defense.

The noise from the next room is laughter, he realizes. His heart leaps. *Vasily!* He flings aside his covers and goes out into the small front room of the flat.

There, Yuna is sitting on the sagging red sofa, dangling a feather on a piece of string just above Misha's head. The cat is pawing at the feather, hoisting himself up on his hind legs to stand like a person. To Artem's astonishment, his mother is sitting in the straight-backed wooden chair across the room, laughing as Yuna bounces the feather for Misha to swipe at. Anna Olegovna sets her teacup down on the end table covered with a blue-and-white embroidered cloth.

Artem had been surprised when his mother had given Yuna the sofa for the night. As with dinner, it had been more of a command than an invitation. They'd been washing the dishes when his mother had said, *You'll stay here tonight.*

Artem had expected Yuna to protest. Surely there were rules at the children's home. Surely the matrons expected their charges to come home at night. But the girl had simply nodded as she dried her bowl and placed it on the tray next to the sink.

His mother is not the type to bring home strays. What is it about Yuna that has so captured her affection?

Artem thinks that maybe Vasily's absence has left a void, and his mother has decided to fill it with this orphan girl. Artem rubs the sleep from the corners of his eyes. He certainly doesn't *dislike* Yuna, but she is hardly his older brother.

"Artem!" his mother says. "Good morning. Open the curtain, will you?"

Two steps bring him to the edge of the sofa. He reaches behind Yuna and slides the faded yellow curtain to one side. Morning light spills into the room, stretching into a bright rectangle along the scuffed wooden floor.

It is then that he notices Yuna is wearing some of his old clothes. Trousers that are slightly too long, rolled at the ankles. And a tan work shirt with its unbuttoned cuffs flopping around her wrists. Why not just give her his favorite forage cap, too? The one that Vasily gave him.

"Misha," he says, slapping his palms on his thighs. "Come here. Let's get you some breakfast."

But the cat just goes on playing with Yuna. With the feather-string toy *he* made.

"All right," his mother says, rising from her chair. "We need to be out the door in five minutes. Artem, there's porridge in the kitchen for you. Don't linger over it."

With that, she rushes into her bedroom. Artem hears drawers opening and closing.

"Hi," Yuna says, setting the feather toy down on the cushion next to her. Misha, triumphant, jumps up to claim it.

"Hi," he says. She meets his eyes. All at once, shame rises. He feels his face getting hot again. The detsky dom is very likely crowded and noisy. Yuna probably sleeps in a room with twenty or thirty other girls. His mother did her a simple kindness by feeding and clothing her, and letting her stay in a quiet room on a clean sofa. "Listen," he says. "I'm sorry I get a little distracted when we're supposed to be working."

"That's okay."

"If I promise to be more helpful, do you think we could talk a little bit?"

"Yes," Yuna says. Then she glances at the bedroom and lowers her voice. "But don't tell your mother. I'm a little bit scared of her."

Artem grins. "She can be a little bit scary. One time she caught my brother, Vasily, stealing a kaleidoscope from the Univermag, and made him go back and tell every store employee that he was a thief."

Yuna's eyes widen. "That place is huge!"

"It took all day."

Yuna laughs. Misha turns over to expose his belly—his way of asking for scratches.

"He likes you," Artem says. "He doesn't do that for everybody."

Five minutes later, the three of them are outside. The bright clear day is already hot—perfect for a picnic on the vast hilltop of the Mamayev Kurgan and a swim in a municipal pool. For a moment he lets the fantasy take over. A day of freedom and discovery, alone with his sketch pad among the cypress trees, ducking into the underbrush to observe a fat little marmot unnoticed . . .

"Artem!" His mother is calling him from up the block. Deep in his reverie, he has stopped walking without even realizing it. He jogs to catch up. Hands on her hips, Yuna shakes her head.

"Off to a good start," she says.

"I know, I know. I'm sorry!"

He forces himself to bring his brother's parting words to the forefront of his mind, imagines tacking them to the front of his skull, just behind his eyelids. *No more time for hobbies. No more time for hobbies. No more time—*

"Attention, comrades!" A loudspeaker perched on a lamppost in front of Petrukhin's corner grocery crackles to life. Artem groans, expecting the standard warning. But this time, the voice says something new. "The Germans are bombing stations northwest of the city." Artem pauses to listen. He thinks he can hear a low, distant rumble. "Citizens should not be alarmed. No air-raid warning has been sounded inside the city."

Artem looks at Yuna. She shrugs. What else is there to do but go to work?

CHAPTER

The Party officials release them early that afternoon. A commissar with a bullhorn makes the announcement.

"It is such a beautiful day, Comrade Stalin himself has authorized the defense work to be suspended. Please return to your homes immediately and enjoy the rest of your evening."

Artem drops his shovel and wipes his brow.

"Phew! I'm exhausted. And my feet are killing me."

Yuna laughs. "That's because you actually worked a full day today."

Artem reflects on this. His first instinct is to protest, but he figures she's probably right. He decides that he's proud of himself. They carried on a conversation, and he didn't once get lost in the skies, tracing the migration of beautiful red-footed falcons, even though he caught their V-shaped formation out of the corner of his eye and nearly gasped in delight.

Yuna reaches into the pocket of her—or, rather, *his*—trousers and produces a red-and-gold foil-wrapped candy.

"Vzletnaya!" Artem exclaims. "I must have left one in those pants last time I wore them."

She reaches into the other pocket and comes up with a second.

"One for each of us," he says. She hands him the candy. As he unwraps it, Artem's fingers are instantly covered in half-melted red goo. He pops it into his mouth anyway and the tartness stings his cheeks. "My brother loves these."

He wonders if the frontoviki have any candy to eat.

Suddenly, he freezes. It didn't occur to him until now, but he has no idea where his brother is stationed. Could he be in the northwestern districts of the city, holding the line out beyond the massive factories?

Could the Nazi bombs be dropping on Vasily right now while Artem stands here with Yuna eating cherry Vzletnaya?

"Let's go," his mother says, coming up behind them. "We must hurry."

There's tension in her voice that takes him away from thoughts of his brother. Artem gazes to the south, where the shadows of the petroleum tanks fall across the wide, placid Volga. Hundreds of workers move across the disturbed earth with great urgency, heading for the streets of the central district. This is not the usual orderly commute. It's more like a desperate rush.

Grabbing Artem and Yuna, Anna Olegovna practically drags them along with her.

"Um," Artem says, "maybe we can stop by the park on the way home? Not because I want to sketch the squirrels or anything. I didn't even bring my sketchbook. I just wanted to show Yuna—wait, is she coming home with us again? Not that I don't want her to, but—"

"Artem," his mother says quietly, in the low voice that means she is particularly stressed, "you're twelve years old. You have to *listen* to what the commissars are actually saying."

She leads them out through a makeshift gate. The city begins to take shape around them in wide boulevards full of oddly spaced structures—the edge of a metropolis trickling out toward the river in one direction and rising in the other.

"'Return to your homes immediately,'" his mother says, repeating the words from the announcement. "Does that sound like Comrade Stalin is dismissing us out of the kindness of his heart? Because it's such a beautiful day? Because he wants us all to picnic on the Mamayev Kurgan?"

"It sounds like they want to clear the streets," Yuna says.

"Correct," Anna Olegovna says, ushering them down a side street that curls into a narrow alley behind a bathhouse. "Because something is coming."

"Then why don't they just tell us what it is?" Artem says.

"So we don't panic," Yuna guesses.

"Maybe," his mother says as they emerge from the mouth of the alley onto a cobbled street Artem doesn't recognize. "Or maybe they're just so used to half-truths they can't help it."

As if on cue, the mournful howl of the siren rises up from the city like a slow-moving flock of herons taking flight. This time there is no voice from a loudspeaker informing citizens of an air raid in some other part of the city. There is only the siren.

Artem's heart pounds. All around him, people are breaking into full sprints, skidding around corners and into doorways. It's as if the city itself is quivering in anticipation.

"Come on!" Artem's mother calls out. She gives them a quick glance to make sure they're following. Then she breaks into a run, barreling forward like a bull down the sidewalk.

They take a hard left turn onto a street Artem knows. There's the old corner store with the faded dolls in the window, the druggist that keeps the bear-shaped chocolates in a bin behind the counter, the workers' supply depot with its worn-out fence. They are still so far from home! The central district is enormous, with endless overlapping neighborhoods. Keep going south and eventually the brick buildings are replaced by wooden houses and shacks until there's nothing at all, only the empty steppe.

"Oof!" Artem is half spun around as he collides with a middle-aged man hurrying past. Yuna grabs his arm to keep him upright.

"Thanks!" he huffs.

Everyone is scattering like cockroaches when you turn on the light, he thinks. *Millions of us, scrabbling blindly for safety as the sirens wail. Or, no, we're more like ants, with our little mazes and tunnels, built through the collective labor of the workers and peasants, while—*

"Artem!"

This time it's Yuna breaking his reverie. She's still gripping his arm, pulling him along. "Look!" She points up into the vast western sky at a swarm of tiny black dots—hundreds of them, as if the lens of the world has become saturated with dust. He manages to run along, keeping an eye on the awful blemish in the sky.

A strange silence descends. Even though the streets are still crowded with people racing to find shelter, all he can hear is the shrill rise and fall of the siren. Nobody screams or cries out. Everyone runs with mouths set in grim lines, eyes wide, herding their children.

Overhead, before Artem can comprehend how fast they are moving, the swarm of dots becomes a thousand aircraft in tight formation. A loudspeaker blaring a siren comes and goes next to his head. The noise is deafening—and then it is behind him. He's aware of a family off to his left as the mother trips and the children end up in a heap at her back. The German planes are defined shapes now, wings and tails and swastikas. They move as one great mass, almost as if they're pinned to the air and the sky is moving behind them. Artem can't look away. They are close enough now to separate them into distinct sizes.

Several things happen at once. The gun batteries across the river open up. Shells pour into the sky, explosions like thudding fireworks as each one bursts. At the same time, a series of smaller gull-winged bombers nose down and plummet straight toward the city. An unholy shriek drowns out the air-raid siren, the whine of a million mosquitoes amplified and pumped directly into his ears. Cold fear forms in a knot between his eyes and flows down into his entire body.

Stukas.

German dive-bombers.

The Luftwaffe has just unleashed their most fearsome weapon on Stalingrad. On his home.

Even through his terror, Artem is struck by the incredible sight. As the antiaircraft fire pops harmlessly above them, the Stukas scream down toward the city at breathtaking speed. People scatter. The bombers pull up as their bombs fall. It's as if they used their incredible speed to fling bombs straight down into the city.

The impact shakes the streets. Glass shatters. The Stukas arc up into the sky through a blanket of cloudbursts. Even here, at the eastern edge of the central district, Artem can see smoke billow up from the explosions.

His mother turns and pulls Artem and Yuna around a corner, into an alley that stinks of fish scraps and oil.

"Mom!" Artem yells, pulling back, turning her around.

The fierce look on her face is almost a sneer. "We have to keep going!"

His brother's words echo. *Take care of our mother.*

"We'll never make it all the way home," he says, shouting to be heard over the sirens and the shriek of the Stukas and the dull roar of the larger bombers coming in behind them. "We need to find a cellar."

"All right," she agrees.

The ground shakes as another round of bombs comes down upon the city. Yuna thrusts out an arm to steady herself against the weather-beaten brick wall. A few more paces down the alley they find the flat metal trapdoors that typically lead to a shop's storage cellar.

Artem's mother bends down, grips the handle, and throws open the doors. Frantic cries spill up out of the darkness.

"Close the doors!"

"There's no more room here!"

"Find someplace else!"

Anna Olegovna leans down to shout into the cellar. "I have children with me! Let us in!"

The voices inside swell to a fever pitch. A hairy-knuckled hand appears and grips the inside latch of the metal doors. Anna leaps back as the hand yanks the doors shut with a sharp *clang,* muffling the voices inside.

"Come on!" This time it's Yuna rushing to the mouth of the alley. She leads them across a wide avenue with a grassy median toward a stairwell under the front stoop of an apartment block, where the building's trash collects. Artem notes how quick she is, like a darting chipmunk as she heads for the concrete eaves. In the window of a first-floor apartment, a set of *matryoshka* dolls are lined up from large to small.

The bright afternoon darkens suddenly. Artem feels the shadows come across the avenue and hears the whine of engines. Without looking up he knows that the bombers are overhead, blotting out the sun. How strange and awful to be invaded from the air. He feels the sting of it acutely, the terror and helplessness, and a rage like he's never known throbbing in his head. It's all happening so fast. Just a few minutes ago he was putting down his shovel for the day. Sitting with Yuna while she dangled Misha's feather toy. Saying goodbye to his brother in Lenin Square. Tagging and releasing a field mouse with Dr. Petrovsky.

He doesn't understand what's happening. It can't be real. Time slows. He feels faint.

It is the smell that brings him back to reality. Acrid smoke and dust filling his lungs, roiling like a low cloud across the avenue.

Yuna is only a few paces from the stoop now. Artem throws a quick glance over his shoulder to make sure his mother is right behind.

The street bucks up and down as if a giant fist has just punched up from the center of the earth. Artem loses sight of Yuna as he's tossed aside by the vicious interruption of the ground itself.

Cutting through the din of sirens and engines and exploding shells and bomb blasts, Artem can hear the delicate, high-pitched shattering of glass.

Every window in the apartment block blows outward. He is on his side, numb from the impact, as glass from a hundred windows pours out into the air like shimmering fragments of ice. Crystals rain down. He shields his face and squeezes his eyes shut. Tiny stings sear his forearm. He risks opening one eye. The headless egg-shaped body of a broken matryoshka—the largest one, he thinks—comes to a skittering stop on the pavement in front of him. Nearby someone is screaming a name he can't make out. He sucks in a breath and gets a mouthful of grit. Coughing, he staggers to his feet.

"Mom!" His throat is sandpaper. "Yuna!"

Through the smoke he catches a glimpse of the apartment block. Bricks hang in tatters from bent steel rods. What he had always taken for granted as solid is suddenly as soft as fabric.

"Artem!" Yuna's voice comes from somewhere ahead.

He stumbles forward. A hand reaches out and takes him by the arm. A moment later his face is inches from Yuna's. An angry red wound runs from one side of her grimy forehead to the other. Plaster and dust are caked in her hair. The skin around her left eye is puffy and swollen.

They look at each other, wordlessly confirming that they are both alive. Somewhere in the swirling, thickening dust, a voice screams nonsense.

Artem tries to call out for his mother and doubles over into a coughing fit.

"Keep going!" His mother's voice, somehow as clear as ever, cuts through the sirens and smoke. A moment later she is pulling him forward, upright and strong, a shifting blur through the haze. Artem rubs grit from his eyes and tries to focus on the world around him. The nightmare that used to be the central district. "Keep going," she says again.

Artem's heart races. He thinks something might be wrong with his mother, the way she is pulling him without looking back. Her body is jerking oddly with each step, her right arm swinging like it's barely attached, bent at a strange angle.

"You're hurt!" he tries to say, but it comes out choked and garbled. Artem knows that he is hurt, too, that there will be pain eventually.

Other dim figures come and go through the cloud of dust, appearing and then vanishing without a word, stumbling blindly around streets they used to know. Artem sees them as fragments of people: hair and teeth and fingers and legs, coming and going.

Then there are stairs. Some kind of ruin above their heads: exposed girders and chunks of cement. His mother ushers them down into a dark hollow. It's impossible to tell what kind of structure it once was. The basement of a store?

The dust is thinner down here, and Artem and Yuna gulp as much air as they can. He pulls a thin spike of broken glass from between his knuckles and tosses it away.

"You're okay," his mother says. She embraces Artem and Yuna, positions her body over them. It's nearly suffocating. "You're okay," she says again. "I'm here."

Artem wonders if their apartment is nearby. He's entirely turned around. For all he knows they could have been running back toward the Volga. He tries not to think of Misha, and then Misha is all he can think about.

The ringing in his ears makes it hard to tell if the siren is still howling across the city. A new sensation rises: heat, powerful and close.

The central district is burning.

Artem sends a silent wish to Misha, that he find his way to a safe spot too small for humans. Some cat-sized hole with a strong roof. At the same time, the awful piercing whine of a diving Stuka comes straight at them. He imagines the German plane bearing down on their heads, the Nazi pilot spotting his mother's red kerchief through the haze and taking aim. There is a chorus of Stukas now, all of them diving in unison, bringing fire and death down upon the city. A dreadful harmony of screaming mosquito engines. How can they ever hope to defend the motherland against this kind of onslaught?

He thinks he can hear the exact moment the Stukas release their bombs. A shift in air pressure, a little click in his mind. His mother squeezes tight and he gasps for air. The world goes dark before he hears the explosion. Then he feels nothing.

CHAPTER

SEPTEMBER

"Germans and Russians. Perhaps not so different in the mind, eh?"

The German officer, an *oberst* in the Wehrmacht, taps a finger against his temple. Artem's eye catches the silver eagle on the man's peaked visor cap, the swastika clutched in its talons. He regards the man's pale, snub-nosed face, with its penetrating blue eyes, sideburns cropped as if with a straight razor, and puffy jowls at odds with his prominent cheekbones. The oberst looks both well scrubbed and well rested, even though he, too, has been living in the devastated ruins of the city in the three weeks since the bombs fell.

"*Mein führer* would not agree, I do not think. So let us keep this talk between us."

Artem is afraid. Until today, he has managed to survive unnoticed by the German soldiers who now occupy his neighborhood. Just another filthy Soviet urchin scrounging for food, haunting the shadows of the district's skeletal remains. He has been isolated by language—the Germans who skulk around shouting their guttural commands might as well be aliens. But now he has been brought before this officer, every inch the strutting Nazi of his nightmares, and this man can speak to him in *Russian*.

The German officer smiles. His smooth face does not wrinkle in the slightest. "You are surprised? I lived for a time in Prague before the war. Many Russian girls there." He winks. "Very beautiful. The city, too." He pauses. "They tell me your Stalingrad was once beautiful." He shrugs. "A shame I only ever saw it after it was . . ." He trails off and gestures around his makeshift officer's bunker, carved out of the wreckage of a bathhouse. "Like this."

They are in one of the new structures defined by ruin. A reshaped part of the city that did not exist before the bombs fell. It is nearly impossible to tell what it once was. Cracked tiles form a wall and part of the floor, as if they are standing at the bottom of one of the baths. Yet their heads are covered by a low ceiling of tin and wooden planks. Artem's not sure if these are from the building's cave-in, or if they've been placed there as protection by the Germans. To enter, he was escorted through a shallow trench—what everyone is now calling a *rat run*—to a blanket hanging over the entrance, flanked by a pair of machine guns poking out over piles of sandbags.

The oberst picks up a shiny object from his desk and steps toward Artem. He stands directly beneath the single bare bulb dangling from lines strung across the ceiling. The light deepens the shadows from his visor. His eyes gleam from the darkness like two icy blue stones. He reaches out a hand. Artem flinches.

"I will not hurt you," he says as his hand moves slowly toward Artem's face. Artem's insides go cold as the man gently traces the mostly healed and scabbed-over wound that runs from Artem's forehead down the bridge of his nose, curls beneath his eye, and slashes down his cheek. "From our bombs, yes?"

Artem nods. The oberst drops his hand. He shakes his head as if he is genuinely pained to learn this.

"You are full of luck. You have your eyes."

Artem shrugs. He certainly doesn't feel lucky. He flashes to his mother and pushes the thought away. Where was luck when Anna Olegovna needed it?

"It will leave a scar." The oberst smiles. "Something to tell the girls about someday."

The bulb flickers and goes out. Artem's heart pounds. The bunker is pitch-black, except for a few small gaps in the planks overhead where light from the ashen sky leaks in.

The oberst makes an irritated *tut-tut* sound. Artem can hear the engine of a single plane, the crackle of flames, the scattered *pop pop pop* of distant rifle fire. The new sounds of Stalingrad that have replaced the sparrows and the bullfrogs.

"Like your unfortunate injury," the oberst says, "this is also our fault. Our bombs cut your main power lines."

Artem knows this. Everyone knows this. The bombs destroyed everything. He is still no closer to understanding why he has been summoned here.

The light comes back on. "Ah!" The oberst cocks his head. "German engineering." He pauses. "Now. Germans and Russians. We are both led by great men. Great men who are very stubborn. Perhaps that is part of the reason for their greatness. And these men think alike, no?

Hitler has ordered us to take Stalingrad. We cannot move from this place until the city falls. We cannot go around it. And Stalin has ordered you all to stay put. He believes your men will fight harder if their women and children are trapped here."

Everyone knows this, too. Stalin has reinforced his Order Number 227—*not one step back*—with another command: No citizens may leave Stalingrad. There are no boats ferrying women and children across the Volga.

"So!" the oberst continues. Artem shuffles his feet. The wound on his face, which he's barely noticed for several days now, has begun to throb as if it's tuned to the frequencies of this stifling bunker. He resists the urge to scratch his cheek, to pick at the scab. "Retreat for either of us means death. In fact, my men have come across piles of dead Red Army soldiers that we did not kill. Do you know who killed them?"

Artem knows. He tries not to think of Vasily. He focuses on the object in the oberst's hand. A brass cylinder the size of a large cup. *A shell casing,* he thinks.

"Your Red Army blocking detachments." The oberst answers his own question. "Men with guns stationed behind the lines to kill those who run from battle. We have our cowards, too, of course. Another thing mein führer would not like to know about. You did not hear it from me." He mimes zipping his lips. "So now we have Germans and Russians, alike in mind, also alike in body. And what does the body need more than anything?"

He turns the hollow cylinder over. A single drop of liquid falls to the dirt.

"Water," Artem says. His heart sinks. Now he knows why he has been summoned here.

"The German Sixth Army is well supplied," the oberst says. He gestures at a crate of wine in the corner of the bunker. "We even have comforts." He walks to the desk, plunks down the shell casing, shuffles some papers and maps, and retrieves half a sausage link from the clutter. He tosses it to Artem. "Please."

Artem's stomach rumbles. He is nearly faint with hunger. Still, he hesitates.

The oberst rolls his eyes. "It is not poison, I assure you. If I wanted to kill a Russian boy, I would simply have you shot."

Cautiously, Artem lifts the sausage to his mouth. In ordinary times it would not be very appetizing. Half a dry link that's been sitting on a desk for who knows how long. But now that he lives on scraps, it's like a feast has just been laid before him. He takes a bite. The flavor is heavenly. He tries to go slow, to savor it, but ends up devouring it in three seconds.

"It is very simple," the oberst says. "When we try to fill up our bottles at the river, your soldiers shoot us."

He goes to the blanket that hangs over the entrance to the bunker, pulls it aside, and barks a command at someone Artem can't see. A moment later, a young woman brings in two canvas packs and sets them down inside the bunker. She doesn't speak a word, but when her eyes flick briefly to Artem, he knows in his heart that she's Russian—a traitor serving this German officer. The oberst waves her away, then reaches inside one of the packs. He produces a metal canteen and tosses it to Artem, who turns it over in his hands. A Nazi eagle like the one on the oberst's cap is printed in the metal.

The oberst lays a hand on Artem's shoulder. "Perhaps they will not shoot a Russian boy. Or perhaps they will." He shrugs. "I suppose we will find out."

CHAPTER

Artem sets the pack full of German canteens down gently, so the clatter won't wake his mother. Even deep in a feverish sleep, Anna Olegovna has a tendency to jolt herself awake at any small noise. Artem does, too, his mind constantly on alert for German patrols.

They are everywhere now.

After the bombs let up, the Panzer tanks had rolled into the city. Except what they rolled into was not really a city anymore. Once the Stukas and the larger Heinkels were finished with Stalingrad, the city had been turned into charred ruins. Now the sky is black with smoke from the ravaged fuel tanks, and the petroleum spreads like a field of fire across the river. Broken smokestacks preside over acres of demolished buildings. Entire rail yards have been twisted into sculptures forged by a madman. Headless statues crumble into smashed fountains. Hanging over it all is a ghostly haze of ash and smoke.

"Are you all right?" His mother's voice is raspy and soft. Artem goes to the filthy mattress on the floor of their shelter. He kneels down to inspect the bandages wrapped around her head. They are soiled and stuck to her skin with dried blood. He has struggled to keep them clean, as there are no fresh ones to be found anywhere—not for Russians who now live behind the German lines.

Lines that are advancing steadily east across the remains of the city, pushing the Red Army back into the river.

He composes his face in the light from the oil lamp so that his mother won't see him grimace at the smell. He takes a look at the makeshift splint he's fashioned for her broken leg: two planks of wood bound together with rope.

The sight of it makes him feel ashamed. The best he can do is not nearly good enough. He is failing at the task his brother entrusted him with.

"I'm fine," Artem says. No matter what happens out in the ruins, this is what he reports to his mother. What point is there in worrying her when she's helpless?

"I dreamed that Vasily flew away on the back of a giant bird," she says distantly, "all the way to the Urals."

"He didn't take us with him?"

There's a long pause. Somewhere, a lost dog barks. *Germans on the move,* Artem thinks. He has come to read the signs of the city like a magician with a crystal ball. Patrols spook the dogs. They spook the people, too: Living in an occupied district means that German soldiers routinely sweep the rubble in search of Russians to ship back to the Reich for slave labor. And one of the occupiers' first orders was for Jewish citizens to wear yellow stars on their sleeves.

"He couldn't find us down here," his mother says. There is great sadness in her voice. *Here* is a network of abandoned trenches in the courtyard of their old apartment building, which now lies in heaps of broken concrete. The entire street looks the same, except for a single chimney that somehow survived, rising like the lone tree on a desolate steppe. Lost possessions dot the ruins like fallen leaves, little pops of color in the drab and lifeless gray world: iron bed frames and knitted quilts, cracked lamps and soup spoons. A stuffed beaver with a great floppy tail sitting upright on a broken chair. Photos in frames of the dead and the lost.

Artem looks around their little cave and tries to remind himself that they are luckier than many of their neighbors. They survived the bombs, and they have a roof over their heads, a place to stay out of sight. He thinks of the oberst's words. *Lucky.* He shakes his head. Outside, the dog goes quiet. He listens for footsteps. Far away, artillery pounds some other sector of the city. A machine gun rattles.

He goes to the child's desk—their single piece of furniture besides the mattresses—and retrieves the leather wineskin. It's an antique that had belonged to one of their neighbors. Now that the city has no electricity or running water, the old wineskin is his prized possession, as if he were living a hundred years ago. He tilts the spout over his mother's cracked lips. A few drops of water spill out.

She clamps her mouth shut. "Save some for yourself."

"It's gone." He tosses the wineskin back onto the desk. "I'll get us more as soon as it gets dark." He glances at the pack in the corner of their shelter. Inside are a dozen canteens imprinted with swastikas.

"Artem," she says. He turns to meet her eyes. He knows what's coming and steadies himself. "You must leave me here. Find a way out. Go east." A dreamy quality laces her voice. "Like your brother and his bird."

Artem squeezes his eyes shut to hold back a surge of shame. His mother, fading in and out of her fever, sweating and bleeding and lying here while he can do nothing but watch.

She grabs his wrist. "Go," she implores.

He opens his eyes. "There's no way out. Stalin said—"

Her grip tightens. "There must be a way! If only I could walk, I . . ." Her eyelids flutter. Gently, Artem pulls his arm from her grasp. "There are networks," she says. "An underground. There is always a way." She pauses again. "Nikolai. Nikolai Gregorovich. From the third floor. He will know."

Artem sighs. "Nikolai Gregorovich is dead." He has explained this to his mother before. He worries that her fever is stealing her memories. He watches her drift into an uneasy half sleep, then goes to the "doorway" of their shelter: a piece of greasy canvas nailed to a crossbeam. He suspects the shelter was originally supposed to be a small officers' quarters, an offshoot from the main trench. Either way, it had been quickly dug by the advancing Germans and then abruptly abandoned.

The German Sixth Army probably expected more of a fight. They thought they'd be dug in all over the city. They hadn't expected to push the Russians back to the river so quickly.

He brushes the canvas aside and steps out into the main trench, a narrow slit in the ground that crosses the courtyard from east to west. Above, the sky is the same color as the earth, as if it is reflecting the dead city. The air smells like he's living in a smoldering fire. He climbs to the fourth rung of a wooden ladder and peeks above the rim of the trench. The remains of his devastated apartment block lie in lumps of concrete and scraps of wallpaper and paint.

"Misha!" He calls in a low singsong hiss. *"Misha-cat!"*

Artem hasn't seen Misha since the first bombs fell. Every time he calls the cat's name, he waits for a blur of black-and-white energy to leap from some secret hidey-hole and bound across the ruins. And every time: nothing. A moment later, he spots a different kind of movement. The careful, deliberate motion of a small human picking her way across the courtyard, glancing this way and that. He watches her oddly deliberate scampering, the way she moves like an upright stick bug. He thinks, not for the first time, that Yuna was made for this environment. She has adapted better than any of them to their dreadful new reality.

He moves aside so she can climb down the ladder.

"No sign of him," she says as her shoes hit the dirt. "But I found this!"

In her hand is a tin can with a white label—German rations. Artem can't read the funny letters, but he knows by their shape that the can contains bratwurst. He has seen this one before.

He raises an eyebrow. "You *found* it?" He imagines Yuna sneaking into one of the German machine-gun nests that bristle from the collapsed walls.

"Just sitting there for the taking," she says.

Artem shakes his head. Except for a few scratches, Yuna survived the bombing unscathed. Maybe she really is lucky.

The wound on his face begins to throb. He thinks of the oberst and the pack full of Nazi canteens inside their shelter.

"We're about to have a lot more of those ration tins," he says. "I made a deal."

She looks puzzled. "With who, one of the Fritzes?"

Artem nods. "An officer."

"Oh no. Artem. What did you do?"

CHAPTER

The department store is a mess of severed pipes sticking up like a half-built church organ. Spindly segments of an upper floor teeter into oblivion just above their heads. Beyond the ruins, dusk darkens the sky. Artem and Yuna follow the black smoke from the burning fuel tanks, the beacon that says *this way to the river.*

They each shoulder a pack as they make their way through the rubble. They've divided the canteens in two to make carrying them easier. Full of water, they will be too heavy for one person.

"So this German officer spoke *Russian* to you?" Yuna asks.

Artem steps carefully over a shattered glass jewelry case. "Yes. The deal is, I get fresh water for his men, he gives me ration tins and fresh bandages. He said if this goes well, he'll even give me a little morphine for my mother's pain."

Yuna makes a disgusted noise. "A deal with a Nazi."

Artem feels his face get hot. "He *could* have said, do this job or I'll kill you, but he didn't. He offered me something in return. I would be dumb not to take it."

Yuna mutters under her breath. Artem keeps his mouth shut, but he can feel anger rising. It's easy for her to criticize his decision—it's not *her* mother lying helpless in a hole in the ground. She doesn't even *have* a mother.

Some deep and shameful part of him envies her this. Maybe that's why she's adapted to the horrors of this new Stalingrad more easily—there's nobody for her to worry about except herself. He hears the oberst's voice echo in his mind: *lucky, lucky, lucky.* He shakes his head, chases it away.

Artem halts at a sudden noise. He puts up a hand to signal Yuna to stop, and he can feel her breathing on the back of his neck. She almost plowed right into him. He stands motionless next to what used to be a grand staircase to the department store's second floor, where children's clothes were arranged in neat sections, along with a little booth selling fizzy water with syrup.

The Sokolovs couldn't afford to shop there, but every now and then, as a special treat, their mother would take Artem and Vasily for one of the sugary drinks. The memory stuns him—so beautiful in its normalcy. He can almost feel the bubbles tickling his nose . . . but he forces himself to focus on the problem at hand. The shifting of debris and the sounds of rummaging and sneaking around that come from everywhere and nowhere.

Artem crouches down, listening, careful not to jostle the pack and rattle the canteens. Yuna makes herself impossibly small at his side. He can't figure out how she does it. She catches his eye and nods toward the store's western entrance, where the big UNIVERMAG sign collapsed and broke in two. Artem listens for a moment, then shakes his head. He nods toward the east, where the store once emptied out in sight of the hills along the riverbank.

Yuna's eyes go wide. Artem's heart pounds. They both realize what's happening at the same time. They are *both* right. Artem sidles over to a stack of toppled shelves. Charred shoes peek out from beneath them. Together, Artem and Yuna hide as best they can.

A moment later, the Germans appear. A small patrol, six of them moving in the low stooped walk of the extremely wary. They are close enough for Artem to make out the lead man's hand signals. Five of them carry rifles, the sixth a long tubelike weapon with a hose attached to a rectangular backpack.

"Flamethrower," Yuna whispers. Artem holds his breath. The fearsome infantry weapon is used to clear bunkers, to roast anybody hiding inside. His eyes flick to a fire-blackened shoe, its leather crisped and brittle. Just a few short weeks ago, he could have come here and walked among racks of shiny new footwear.

The Germans fan out in a new formation, sweeping what's left of the store. Artem listens hard. The sounds from the east have died away. Are they all alone with the Germans? He lifts his head slightly, risks a look above the toppled shelves.

No.

Off to the right, he can see a Red Army soldier ducking behind the remains of a pillar. His eyes search the dim wreckage. Another soldier crouches behind a kitchen table resting on its side, taking aim with his rifle.

Just yesterday, the old department store had been squarely in the German occupied zone. Today it is a battleground. The city as Artem knew it might be dead, but its jagged boundaries are very much alive, and ever shifting.

Artem does a grim mental calculation. If the Russians find them first, they will discover bags full of German army canteens and shoot them for being traitors.

If the Germans find them first, they will shoot them for being thieves before Artem can say the word *oberst*. Or simply burn them out of their hiding spot with that flamethrower.

This is life in Stalingrad now. Impossible choices that lead to the same brutal end. It is a strange feeling that ignites further shame. He wants the Germans to lose, of course. They invaded the motherland. But some deep, dark part of him wonders if it really matters at all.

It is the same for the soldiers. Advance through this ruined department store on some pointless mission and get killed by the enemy. Retreat, and get killed by the people who ordered them here in the first place.

A quick blur catches his eye, the flight of a small object. The *plink* as it hits the cracked floor and rolls toward the German patrol.

"Down!" he hisses. Artem and Yuna curl up.

One of the German soldiers yells. Then the grenade explodes. Artem feels the thud in his stomach, followed by the rush of heat that jets across the top of their hiding place. Rifle fire erupts.

Yuna reaches for his hand. If they stay behind these shelves they will be out of the line of fire. But they can't hide here forever. And if they wait till the firing stops, they will have to cross the rest of the floor, exposed to whichever side is still alive.

There is only one thing to do. He meets Yuna's eyes and gestures toward the rubble at the eastern edge of the store. Beyond that is the cratered earth and jagged remains of the fuel tanks leaking oily smoke. He points. She nods.

Another grenade explodes. The ground shakes. A German soldier cries out. Artem's entire body is screaming for him to *stay put*. It is something he never had to think about before. The instinct to hide, to avoid danger, is powerful. All animals have it, of course. But now he knows he is no different from any of them, from the rats in the trenches to the beasts of the steppe. To get up and go when the world sounds like it's crashing down around you requires great power. It's like telling a bird to fight its instinct to migrate to warmer climates when winter comes. He thinks of the cranes, lingering on the balcony above Lenin Square. Like an open door letting a crack of light into a darkened room, a tiny piece of calm washes over him.

"Now!"

He grabs his pack and pulls Yuna along with him, staying low until they reach the edge of the shelves. There are boots here, a splatter of leather torn apart by a bomb blast. Women's shawls, filthy and torn, litter the ground. He peeks across the smoky expanse. His eyes pick out tiny explosions of plaster and cement where bullets strike debris. Ahead, toward the edge of the store, a half-ruined wall still stands, its three window holes gaping. Artem signals toward the wall.

Off they go.

They run hard toward a burnt mound of clothing. He stops short when he sees the charred limbs. An arm and a leg, poking out of the pile.

Yuna shoves him from behind. "Only mannequins!" she shouts. Artem keeps going, still sickened by the sight of the fake limbs.

A man steps out of the haze just ahead of them. Artem's mind races. Red Army—he can tell by the helmet. The soldier raises his rifle and aims at Artem's head. He puts up his hands.

"Don't shoot!" he screams. "I'm Russian!" This should go without saying—there are no German children in Stalingrad—but it's the first thing that pops into his head.

From behind, Yuna grabs his shoulders and takes him down to the ground with all her weight. They collapse in a heap as the bullet whizzes above them. Artem's head whips around in time to see the German soldier fall. Then the Red Army man melts back into the smoke.

Together, they scramble up with their packs and make for the wreckage of the wall. The sounds of the battle fade behind them. Ahead, black smoke blankets the sky. It's a horrible sight for a beacon, but everything in Stalingrad is ominous now. Even salvation.

CHAPTER 11

The Germans have pushed them back to the river, but the Red Army still holds the landing site on the west bank of the Volga. Just south of the burning fuel tanks, limestone cliffs rise. It's much higher here than the flat eastern side across the water, hidden in the fading light. With darkness falling, the landing zone comes to life. A motley fleet of boats bobs offshore, both military craft and commandeered fishing vessels. Soldiers and workers unload crates of ammunition from a long, flat barge. Briny river smells mingle with the rubbery stench of petroleum and the ash that covers the city.

Artem and Yuna join a group of civilians carrying all manner of jugs and bottles, trudging silently toward the water's edge. They move through a row of sandbagged machine-gun nests defending the landing, manned by dark, suspicious figures with hooded eyes.

Artem tightens his grip on the pack, grateful for the cover of darkness.

All it takes is one Red Army soldier—or worse, a commissar—asking to see their strange load of canteens.

Citizens have been shot for less.

Suddenly, the riverside landing is painted with a bloodred color that glows and then fades. Artem glances up at the sky in time to see a second German flare burst. It comes on like the arc light from a welder, a sun-bright spot shedding its crimson glow.

All around him, the soldiers spring to life, rushing this way and that, training guns on the dark skies. More flares pop. Night becomes a bloody twilight. Artem spies a massive flotilla of boats crossing the Volga from the east bank. He also spots an incredible landing area—multiple docks made from hewn logs, extending like a scaffold out into the river. It is here that the barge is unloading its ammunition. Red Army combat engineers scamper across the docks, making repairs on the fly as the ships come in. Artem can't help but think of all the Sunday afternoons he spent along the river, collecting pale blue eggs and studying fat bull-frogs in their natural habitats. He hopes they have all found their way out of the city.

"Down here," Artem says, leading Yuna into some marshy overgrown grass south of the landing. Nobody pays them any mind. The other civilians scatter to points along the riverbank. One woman pulls handfuls of wrinkled shirts and trousers from an enormous bag and begins dipping them in the water.

"Wait," Yuna says, tugging on his sleeve. She points to an outcrop of the landing beyond the barge. "Look."

A procession of stretchers borne by soldiers is making its way onto a ship. In the eerie light from the flares it looks like something from a dream, mysterious humans in some lonely place conducting an ancient ritual.

"They evacuate the wounded from here," Artem says.

"There must be hundreds of them every night. Thousands, maybe."

Artem's mind churns. "If we could get my mother down here on a stretcher and put her with the others, maybe they would take her aboard."

"We'll have to find a uniform for her to wear as a disguise. Something torn up."

Artem doesn't bother replying. They both know a Red Army uniform from a dead soldier will be easy enough to find. It's just a matter of having the courage to kneel by a corpse long enough to remove it.

The first German shell of the night comes whistling in and splashes into the river. Shells are like roaches: Where there's one, there's a hundred.

"Come on," Artem says. A second shell punches a hole in a fishing vessel. Wood splinters and men dive over the side. Somewhere north of the landing site, a machine gun opens up. He plunks down his pack and looks over his shoulder. There are soldiers milling about, but no one seems very keen to bother two urchins kneeling in the muck.

He takes the first canteen from his pack and dunks it in the river. He gasps as his hand plunges into the ice-cold water of the Volga.

Autumn has only just begun, and his fingers are already numb.

CHAPTER

One week later, the oberst is jubilant. Artem and Yuna stand beside his desk and unpack two dozen canteens full of river water. Grinning, he gives them each a piece of sausage.

"How many times have you been here to this bunker?" he asks.

Artem tries to remember. Fourteen? Fifteen? They've been making the trip to the river once at dusk and once at dawn for the entire week. His confusion lies in whether the pink horizon outside is one or the other—it all runs together, an endless cycle of ashen skies, red flares, thundering artillery, crackling machine-gun fire, and the shouts of the wounded.

"Fifteen," Yuna says wearily. Artem suspects she pretends to be more exhausted than she actually is in the presence of the German officer. It keeps her from having to mumble more than a few words at a time. She refuses to converse with him without being outright defiant.

The oberst folds his arms. His grin remains. He looks from Artem to Yuna and back again. "And? You do not notice anything different?"

Artem takes a bite of the sausage, forces himself to chew slowly and swallow. His stomach is knotted with cramps. He has learned that when you're truly starving, eating too fast can bring blinding pain to your guts.

Yuna finishes silently unloading the canteens from her pack. The oberst picks up each one, testing the weight. While everything else in the city decays and turns to dust, the officer is as freshly scrubbed as ever. Not a hair out of place, not a scuff on his visor cap.

Artem glances around the small bunker. A map tacked to a board shows the shifting front lines, drawn and redrawn as the Germans advance.

"Well?" the oberst prods.

Artem stifles a sigh. These conversations are tiresome, but the oberst seems to like them. And he must try to keep the man happy, for his mother's sake. The fresh bandages and dressings supplied by the German officer are probably saving her life.

"There," Artem says, pointing at a gramophone in the corner behind the desk. A brass horn juts up from the pedestal housing the turntable. It looks expensive. There's barely a scratch on it.

"Winner!" the oberst says, giving Artem a slice of black bread. As soon as the officer turns to the record player, Artem tears off half the piece for Yuna.

There's a muffled scratch as the needle finds its groove. A familiar accordion melody fills the bunker. A moment later, a woman's voice rings out, bold and strong with a hint of playful mischief. Artem looks at Yuna, astonished. The song is "The Little Blue Shawl," a favorite of every Red Army soldier fighting in Stalingrad.

The oberst turns with that grin still plastered to his face and pretends to conduct the music, waving his arms in the air. Then he shrugs.

"It's not Wagner, but what can you do? The Luftwaffe won't be airlifting in German records anytime soon, so we must make do with Russian trifles."

He finishes weighing up the canteens they've delivered, then picks through a crate at the foot of his desk. He tosses a roll of bandages on the desk, then plunks down a stack of ration tins and slides them across to Artem. Yuna turns to leave, but Artem stays put.

The oberst raises an eyebrow. "Yes, boy? Something else I can help you with?"

Artem's heart begins to race. Tension grips him as if he's back in the smoke and chaos of the ruined department store. Back there, he defied his instinct. He can do it here, too. He forces himself to speak. "My mother is in pain. It's getting worse. Her leg isn't setting right."

Yuna pauses at the entrance to the bunker and glances over her shoulder. "Let's go, Artem."

The oberst regards Artem curiously. He taps a finger on the desk. "There are a lot of Germans in pain, too, Artem Romanovich."

Artem winces at the patronymic. Somehow his father's name in this German officer's mouth feels wrong.

"My men are on my mind from the time I wake up till I get a few hours' sleep," the oberst continues. "Wounded men. Dying men. Men who will never again see their homes. Your mother's comfort is not a part of these thoughts. You can understand that. I'm sure, if our situations were reversed, a Red Army officer would not give much thought to a German boy's mother."

Artem tamps down a surge of anger. *The situations aren't reversed,* he thinks, because Russians didn't go marching into the heart of Germany, destroying everything in their path, reducing beautiful cities to rubble.

"We've done everything you asked."

The oberst thinks for a moment. "All right. I can spare three morphine syrettes. Don't ask again."

Artem meets the oberst's eyes. "Thank you."

Yuna looks away in disgust. In this moment, Artem doesn't care what she thinks. He is too relieved to be ashamed. He is going to ease his mother's pain.

The oberst turns to the blanket covering the bunker's entrance. "Natasha!" he calls. The same young Russian woman who dropped off the pack of canteens during Artem's first visit comes bustling in, nearly knocking Yuna to the ground. She is giggling at something a sentry said outside. Artem notes that a German greatcoat is draped across her shoulders. A gaudy necklace sparkles between the open lapels.

"Yes, *herr oberst*?" she says. The German words coming from one of his fellow Russians make Artem feel sick. He is nearly overcome with distaste for this woman, this Russian who serves the German invaders, laughs with their soldiers, jumps at their officers' whims. There are plenty of citizens like her, men and woman who couldn't wait to get cozy with the Nazi occupiers.

Artem tells himself that what *he* is doing is different. He has no choice. His mother will die unless he brings water to the Germans. Plus, he and Yuna will starve. He bears himself up with these thoughts, but at their core is doubt. If a Red Army soldier or commissar saw him here, delivering canteens like a good little errand boy, groveling for a few morphine syrettes, what would they think of him? He would seem no less a traitor than Natasha.

A mortar round explodes nearby. Dust like fine silt shakes loose from the ceiling.

"Do you know where our medic is?" the oberst asks.

"Sleeping, herr oberst."

"Very well. Don't wake him. Open his field pack and fetch me three morphine syrettes."

Artem watches Natasha's face as she nods, eager and smiling. Is this what he looks like, a puppy who can't wait to obey his master's command? He turns away as the Russian woman and the German officer make friendly small talk. The sounds of "The Little Blue Shawl" begin to grate on him. The song is a reminder of noble soldiers like Vasily, singing quietly in their trenches at night, comforted by the wistful melody.

He glances at Yuna. She has turned her back completely and seems to be ducking her head to make herself as small as possible. He watches, puzzled, as she edges farther into the shadows.

Natasha moves to exit the bunker and stops short. She peers at Yuna. As if feeling Natasha's eyes on her, Yuna shrinks even further into herself. A smile of recognition plays at Natasha's bright red lips.

"Yuna," she says at last.

Artem is speechless. The oberst frowns and folds his arms across his chest, watching curiously.

Yuna shakes her head and makes for the doorway.

"Yuna of the pretty brown hair, I'm sure it's you!" Natasha says loudly. Yuna reaches out to part the blanket hanging over the opening.

"Stop!" the oberst commands. Reluctantly, Yuna lowers her hand. She still does not turn around. "Natasha, do you know this girl?"

Natasha steps toward Yuna, lays a rough hand on her shoulder, and spins her around. Yuna keeps her head bowed. Natasha takes a clump of Yuna's hair and tosses it away from her face. Then she puts a finger underneath Yuna's chin and lifts her head. The look of defiance on Yuna's face breaks Artem's heart—it's a brittle thing, with fear creeping around the edges. He wishes he could rush over and pull her through the doorway, out of the bunker, away from this Nazi and his Russian pet. But the only thing waiting for them outside is more Germans with machine guns. All he can do is watch as Natasha looks Yuna in the eyes, a cruel smile curling her mouth.

"Oh yes," Natasha says. "We are old friends from the detsky dom." She squeezes Yuna's shoulder. "Always trouble, this one. A very willful girl, ever since she showed up on our doorstep." She leans in close to Yuna's face. "And the woman who left you there—we all know what *she* was. Don't we?"

Artem imagines taking Yuna by the hand and leading her away from this place, across the river, to some peaceful hideout in the Ural Mountains, like Vasily told him to do back in August.

He failed to protect his mother. And now he's failing to protect Yuna.

Outside, mortar fire picks up. The oberst eyes the ceiling of his bunker with distaste as more dust shakes loose. "This is all very touching." He turns to the gramophone and lifts the needle, silencing the scratched loop. "But I'm afraid I must get back to work."

He pauses as Natasha rushes over, cups her hand around his ear, and whispers. The oberst frowns. Then he looks at Yuna as if seeing her for the first time.

"Well, well. It seems I've been given my very own Jew."

CHAPTER

Artem is alone with the oberst. Natasha has been dismissed, and Yuna marched away by one of the German sentries.

"You must think me a monster, Artem Romanovich," the oberst says. He sits in the creaky chair behind his desk and removes his visor cap. "Taking your friend away like that."

Artem is having a hard time believing that any of this is really happening. He feels like a shabby little copy of the real Artem.

The real Artem would know how to save Yuna. The real Artem would, at the very least, spit some defiant line at the oberst. *This* Artem only knows how to sit helplessly in front of the Nazi who just hauled his friend away.

"Did you know she was a Jew?" the oberst asks.

No, he thinks, *but my mother did*.

Now it all makes sense, why his mother was so protective toward Yuna.

He thinks of the people he's seen among the ruins, scavenging like everyone else—except for the yellow stars the Germans force them to wear. These Jewish citizens tend to be the ones who disappear after a roundup. Sent to the camps out on the steppe, Artem has heard. Either that or loaded into trains and sent west, into the heart of the Reich.

His mother foresaw this terrible future.

"What's going to happen now?" Artem asks. His voice is dry, the words as scratchy as the record.

The oberst stares at him. "That's up to you," he says at last. "I don't hate Jews, you know." He plants his elbows on his desk and leans forward. Artem fights the urge to recoil. "My fellow officers would have Yuna sent straight to one of our work camps, but I think acting out of pure hatred is shortsighted. Don't you agree?"

"I don't know," Artem says. "I don't hate anybody."

The oberst cocks his head. "Not even me?"

Artem is silent. The oberst smiles his infuriating smile. "Well, never mind that. What I'm saying is, it's all well and good to round up enemies and send them to the camps. Perhaps one could make the argument it is in the best interest of the Reich to feed our industry with slave labor." He shrugs. "But I think even this concern is a lesser one than taking Stalingrad." He lowers his voice as if he's telling Artem a great secret. "Stalingrad is the key to Russia, and Russia is the key to this war." He glances at the doorway of the bunker. His voice is a near whisper now. "The sooner this city falls, the sooner I can go home. And I *will* see Germany again."

I hope Stalingrad is your grave, Artem thinks. *You and your entire army.*

He imagines himself saying this to the oberst. What, then, would the man do to Yuna? Have her shipped off to die in a camp? Have her shot in front of him? Shoot them both?

He forces himself to remain composed. He thinks of his mother, and Vasily, and Yuna, and Misha.

He takes a deep breath. "What do you want me to do?"

The oberst's eyes sparkle. He runs a hand through his hair. Then he turns, bends at the waist, and takes the lid off a wooden crate. "You see, Artem Romanovich, this is why I like you."

He straightens up in his chair and sets a hand grenade on the desk between them. Artem has seen grenades like this tucked into the belts of dead soldiers in the streets. A metal cylinder like a small can of beans attached to a wooden stick for a handle. "You are a pragmatist. We can make deals, you and me."

Artem goes cold. His fear is a ball of ice at the base of his spine, freezing him in place.

"You know how to use this?" the oberst asks. Artem shakes his head.

The oberst tilts the grenade so that the stick is facing him. "You simply give this a tug to ignite the fuse." He indicates a little bead protruding from the hollow at the base of the stick. "Then you have four point five seconds until it explodes. Now. What you will do is not so different from filling up the canteens in exchange for rations and bandages. In fact, you'll be going to the same place. The riverbank landing site."

Artem imagines trudging past the hard faces of the Red Army soldiers protecting the landing, tucked into their machine-gun nests. Except instead of suspicious water bottles, he'll have a German grenade.

This is real, he tells himself, though he scarcely believes it. *This is real.*

"There is a barge that comes at night," the oberst continues. "A big flat ship. The biggest one in the whole flotilla. You know it?"

Artem nods. The ammunition delivery.

The oberst slides the grenade across the desk so it rests in front of

Artem. "Light the fuse. Toss the grenade onto the deck of the barge. And run."

Artem reaches out and hefts the grenade. It's heavy. Solid. Deadly. He knows that what the oberst says is true: Before it can explode, the fuse must be lit. There is very little danger in simply holding it. But still he is aware of its pent-up energy. Whenever he touches it, the distance between life and death shrinks a little more. He peers at the script printed onto the metal cylinder.

"German design," the oberst says. "So don't worry. It won't blow up before you tell it to. Our transaction is simple: When I get word that the barge has been destroyed, I will give you back your friend. Understand?"

Artem places the grenade in his pack. He handles it gently as if it is one of the snapping turtles that live in the *balkas*—the ravines running at right angles to the river. "I understand."

"Good!" The oberst leans back in his chair and crosses one leg over the other. "If you fail," he says casually, "Yuna will die in the camps."

Artem shoulders the pack. His voice is gone. The ice has frozen his entire spine. He turns to go.

"Oh. Artem!"

He turns back. The oberst slides a roll of fresh gauze across the table. "For your mother. God bless her."

CHAPTER

The oil lamp casts deep shadows that pool throughout their shelter. Artem unwraps the bandages around his mother's leg. Days ago, he removed the splint, hoping the bones had set. But some kind of infection remains where the bone once protruded from the flesh beneath her knee. He holds his breath—the wound smells bad. He tries to keep his face blank and composed. His mother's unpredictable fever has receded tonight. She is alert on her mattress, and Artem is hopeful.

"The screechers are back," she says. Somewhere far away—maybe the northern tip of the factory district—the Stukas hammer the city with bombs, screaming all the way down. Closer to their neighborhood, on the cratered surface of the Mamayev Kurgan, an artillery barrage thunders. Closer still, in the no-man's-land of the desolate streets, machine guns rattle and spit. The oil lamp gutters in the corner. The shadows deepen. Artem pauses with the bandage half wrapped until the light steadies.

"I barely even hear them anymore," Artem says.

"It shouldn't be this way. A boy your age, getting used to a life like this. This is no life at all. *Ouch!*" His mother curses. Artem freezes. Then he resumes, slowly and gently, until the upper part of her calf, her swollen knee, and her lower thigh are all freshly wrapped. After he stows the rest of the gauze in a small toy chest he found in the wreckage of their building, he mops his mother's forehead with a cloth dipped in rainwater he collected in a tarpaulin.

"The *rasputitsa* is almost here," he says. The season of rain and mud.

"Your father's birthday is coming up," his mother says. Artem dabs water on her cracked lips. "October third. I don't think it was ever dry for his picnic."

Artem wrings the cloth out into a chipped ceramic bowl. "It rained every year and you still had a picnic?"

"He insisted! We'd go to the park, lay out our food on a blanket, and eat while we got soaked." She closes her eyes. "Foolish, foolish man . . ."

Artem turns to his own mattress, brushes dirt from his thin sheet. His eyes flick to the pack in the corner of the shelter. Inside is the German grenade.

"Nikolai Gregorovich," his mother says suddenly.

Artem sighs. Not this again. "He died back in August, remember? In the first bombing. I told you this."

Frustrated, his mother curses. She squeezes her eyes shut, concentrating, then lets out a breath. "His son, I mean. His son is alive."

Artem thinks for a moment. Nikolai had been an old man, and his son must be at least fifty. "Fyodor Nikolaevich," Artem says, pulling the son's name up from the recesses of his mind. He remembers Fyodor's bushy eyebrows and the tilt of his battered hat as they passed on the street outside their building.

"Yes. Fyodor. I heard his violin last night. He is alive, Artem, I know it."

"I hope he is," Artem says, opening one of the German ration tins he's stockpiled under the desk. It smells like liverwurst, a flavor he'd never thought he'd get used to. But when people all over the city are eating rats and squirrels, this can of army food is a luxury. He takes a spoon from the desk drawer and lays a moth-eaten blanket over his stash. Not much protection from a determined scavenger, but at least it's out of sight if someone were to peek in.

"Fyodor is the one you need to talk to, Artem. He will be part of the underground, like his father was. Whatever network has sprung up in what's left of this city."

Artem spoons a bit of the pink meat paste into his mother's mouth. "Talk to him about what?"

His mother swallows, then glares at him. "You know what I'm saying. Don't play dumb."

Artem sighs. "I'm not leaving you."

"Fyodor and his father could get anything on the black market, and they could do it quickly."

"I remember," Artem says. Every now and then they would find Western chocolates slid under their door. He spoons another bite into his mother's mouth. Every time he feeds her, he is struck by how, not so long ago, she was the one feeding him. It's only been twelve years since he was a helpless baby. Twelve years of life before their roles abruptly switched. The sense of wrongness washes over him. He scratches the back of his neck, his shoulders, his chest beneath his shirt.

His mother eyes him suspiciously. "Lice?"

Artem shrugs. "Probably." He gives her a sip of water from the old wineskin and wipes her mouth with a bit of clean gauze. She lifts her arm off the mattress and takes him by the wrist.

"Promise me you'll talk to Fyodor."

Artem looks into his mother's wet, imploring eyes. He thinks of her quiet resolve, her toughness. The mysterious strength that makes her do things like take in an orphan girl during the hardest time the city's ever faced. He longs to ask her about Yuna, about how she knew the girl was Jewish. About how she saw what the Nazis were going to do to the people of this city. Especially to the ones they hate the most.

"All right," he says. "I promise."

"Listen for the violin. He's here somewhere."

Artem turns to stow the rest of the liverwurst for later.

"Where is Yuna this evening?"

He freezes. "Out looking for Misha." The lie hits the air and fouls it. Artem feels a burning need to get out of the shelter before he confesses everything to his mother. He mutters something about going to help and rushes out into the abandoned trench. He braces himself with a hand against a packed dirt wall and waits for a rush of sickness to pass. Then he climbs the ladder up into the scarred city, breathing the black dust of war, calling quietly for his missing cat.

CHAPTER

Artem waits for the rain to come. He doesn't have to wait long. Three days later, Stalingrad is in the thick of the rasputitsa. The torn-up streets become a slurry of jagged pavement floating like icebergs atop a sea of slick mud. Bodies left to rot sink quietly into the muck, gone and forgotten. Still, the constant downpour does nothing to dampen the enemy artillery, or the bombing raids.

It's almost October, and Artem can hardly believe the city still holds. The Germans and the Red Army are dug in, fighting a never-ending, relentless battle over a vast plain of rubble. He moves past a row of blackened German tanks, the burnt husk of a bombed-out fountain, a fallen statue of a winged angel. His overcoat, sized for a grown man and pulled from the wreckage of a tailor's shop, is sodden and heavy. Underneath its folds, the German hand grenade is tucked into his belt.

Somewhere nearby, submachine guns chatter. They are answered by the high-pitched howl of *katyusha* rockets. This is the constant conversation of war, background noise Artem barely hears.

A few short months ago, in the middle of summer, this same roundabout journey to the Volga would have taken him through some fascinating urban habitats. Wrens and sparrows in the linden trees, chipmunks in the community gardens, stray cats on the prowl. With the click of his mind's microscope, he could peer into the complex inner workings of the less prominent species: bees pollinating bright flowers, ants in the cracks of the sidewalk. All of them part of the web that pulses through every corner of the city.

Now he only ever sees rats. Big ones that seem to have grown fatter while the rest of the population starves.

He comes to the end of a street where all that remains of a house is an iron bed frame, a crumbled brick fireplace, and a kitchen chair. It's almost dusk, but it might as well be the middle of the night. The soot-blackened air is like a series of dark curtains rustling all around him.

Suddenly, he ducks down into the half shelter of the fallen hearth without exactly knowing why. The occupied city has given him a sixth sense for danger, something not directly related to hearing or sight. He is an animal in these ruins. A furtive, darting creature.

A moment later, the danger reveals itself. A patrol. Eight Red Army soldiers in a procession, low silhouettes against whatever passes for light in this place. Their rifles glide slowly and automatically, covering their flanks. Artem waits for them to move out of sight. He doesn't want to find out what they would do to a boy carrying a German hand grenade.

Sometime later, he reaches the nearest balka. The deep, narrow trench is lined with command posts and bustling with Red Army activity. Civilians are tolerated, and many of them pass through on their way to fill water bottles or wash clothes in the river. If Artem were on an innocent errand, he would hop down into the ravine. But to do so now would be suicide. For him and Yuna both. Not to mention his mother.

A German flare pops high in the sky, and the familiar crimson glow descends over the riverbank. To the north, the fuel tanks smolder, and the red tint paints the black smoke.

He makes his way south of the ravine, through a landscape of low bracken and prickly scrub.

Suddenly, he stops short, dizzy with a feeling like hunger, but also longing. The smell of freshly baked bread washes over him and nearly brings him to his knees. Images come along with it: lazy Sunday mornings at home, the clink of plates and mugs on the kitchen table, neighbors stopping by for gossip and a bite to eat. Misha in his lap.

Artem moves forward, oblivious to the danger, pulled by the scent. He can't feel his feet. He might as well be floating.

To his astonishment, he comes to a camouflaged lean-to. Under the green tarpaulin, a genuine Russian stove has been half buried in the earth. Several men mill about. One of them dons a pair of heavy gloves and pulls a steaming loaf of bread from an opening in the white bricks of the stove.

Without a plan, Artem finds that he's stepped to the edge of the lean-to. This close to the landing site, these men have to be transport troops. One of them glances up at Artem with amusement.

"Hello, boy. You've stumbled upon the Red Army's top-secret base. Don't tell the Germans we're here."

"You're making bread," Artem says, pointing like a wide-eyed zombie at the stove.

The man laughs. "We've got ourselves a real academician here, gentlemen! Come, come, get out of the rain."

Artem ducks beneath the tarpaulin and marvels at the scene. Russian stoves weigh hundreds if not thousands of kilograms—how did they get it here?

The man watches Artem take it all in and seems to read his thoughts. "We're transport troops and army engineers," he says. "What good are we if we can't transport anything and everything?"

The man wearing gloves sets the newly baked loaf atop the white bricks. Artem has known old men to actually sleep atop their Russian stoves for warmth in winter. It always seemed to him like a habit from a bygone age, when Stalingrad was still called Tsaritsyn and peasants lived in wooden *izba* dwellings. The man pulls off a chunk and tosses it to Artem.

"Hot bread!" he calls out.

Artem juggles the scorching bread in his hands, blowing to cool it down. Then he takes a bite. It's heavenly. Not the stale black hunks he and Yuna bartered for, with crusts so sharp they cut the roof of Artem's mouth. This bread is soft and richly flavored. He closes his eyes and lets it linger on his tongue. It's almost as if he's dissecting it in his mind—the taste of the grain, and there's the flour. He swallows it slowly.

This precious meal has the unfortunate effect of making Artem ravenous. His stomach knots and cramps, but it's worth it. He opens his eyes to find the transport troops all watching him solemnly.

"Is your father at the front, comrade?" one of them asks.

Artem shakes his head. "He died a long time ago. My brother is, though. The Fifty-First Guards Rifle Division."

"Under Semenov," the bread maker says. "Tough bunch. And your mother?"

"She's . . . at home."

The men regard him knowingly. They understand what *home* means in late September in Stalingrad. A burned-out shell of a building or a hole in the ground.

A third man rips off an ample chunk of bread and wraps it in a thin scrap of cloth. Then he steps up to Artem. But instead of handing over the bread, the man reaches for the pocket of his overcoat.

Artem goes numb with fear. If his hand moves three inches to the left, he will feel the outline of the German grenade. Artem stands very still as the man stuffs the bread into the pocket, then claps him on the back. "Relax, boy. It's only war."

The other transport troops laugh. One of them begins kneading dough stretched out on a metal tray. Another pours vodka into empty shell casings.

"I'd better go," Artem says. He points stupidly at the river. "Water."

The man nods, sipping vodka.

"Thank you," Artem says, patting his pocket.

The gloved man bows. "Thank *you* for visiting the best bakery in Stalingrad." Together, they begin to sing "The Little Blue Shawl." Artem heads out of the lean-to. As the ragged chorus fades away behind him, another German flare pops overhead. The smell of the stove is gone, replaced by the familiar stench of the riverbank—fuel and smoke and fire.

Artem stops. The flotilla, spurred to motion by the dying light, has begun its nightly crossing. Red-tinted ships press forward beneath the light of the flares. Soon, German artillery will begin splashing down. Some of the shells will find their marks. Ships will sink. But many will not, and the Red Army will drag its lifeblood ashore—ammunition, food, fresh troops—while the wounded will be sent across in the other direction.

The circulatory system of war.

Artem keeps to the shadows south of the landing site as best he can. He moves along the base of a low hill, keeping the earth between him and the machine-gun nests that ring the landing. The Red Army has become better equipped to defend their positions than they were just a few weeks ago. After all, if the Germans were to take this landing, they would cut off a vital Russian supply line.

Artem knows this is why the oberst is using him. Sabotaging the barge will be a major setback. And it will cost the Germans nothing—not a single solder. What is the life of a Russian boy to them?

Artem moves a hand along the bread and the grenade in turn. Nourishment and destruction. Yet only the grenade can save Yuna.

He steadies himself to slow his racing heart. Staying low, he peers around a mound of dirt at the base of the hill. Some old fortification, half dug and abandoned.

The barge is heading for the landing, low and flat and dark. Artem can see the silhouettes of ammunition crates stacked high, dark towers gliding across the water. On the docks, transport troops gather, waiting to unload the supplies. Artem charts his course to the riverbank. Through the scrub grass, into the muck at the river's edge, waist-deep in frigid water to get past the sentries with their guns . . .

He waits for the latest flare to burn itself out. The crimson glow dims. The rain dies away, leaving a cool humidity in its wake. He pulls his forage cap low and leaves the relative safety of the hillside to move through patchy foliage, hardy grasses that even the churn of bombs and boots can't kill. His shoes suck at earth the consistency of soft glue. His blood rushes in his ears. He thinks of the men in peacetime ambling back from the Volga with their day's catch of freshwater sturgeon. Delicious.

Artem comes to the ragged edge of a wire fence. To get around it, he wades in the river up to his ankles. The shock of the cold is like a frozen hammer blow. Icy water soaks his battered shoes, claws at his calves. Dull numbing pain rises up his legs. He clamps his mouth shut to keep his teeth from chattering and moves slowly, so as not to splash. Just ahead, the barge pulls up to the floating pier made of logs stripped and lashed together by the Red Army engineers. Sailors toss lines to troops on the shore.

Artem creeps forward until he's huddled in the place where the pier meets an earthen wall, rising above the riverbank. It's like being shoved into the crook of an elbow. Five meters away, the barge bobs in the water. He can see the low choppy waves lapping at the ship's corroded hull.

Inside his coat, the grenade moves with the pounding of his heart. He unbuttons the coat, reaches in, and pulls the grenade out of his belt. A box of ammo is passed from ship to shore. Artem watches the men bustling like ants in a colony as he clutches the handle of the grenade in his sweaty fist. The river smells of dead fish and brine. His senses are open; blood pounds in his temples.

His fingers close around a bead at the base of the handle. Pulling this will tug the string that ignites the fuse. Then it's just a matter of a simple heave, the grenade spinning end over end, plunking down on the deck of the barge. The ammunition will go up in the explosion—thousands of rounds packed with flammable black powder. The explosion will kill everyone on board and half the men on the pier. The Germans will hear the sound all the way back in the streets of the central district. The oberst will lean back in his chair and smile to himself. *It is done.*

And then what? Yuna will go free if the oberst keeps his word. A big *if,* Artem thinks. And it won't just be his fellow Russians at the landing site he's murdering. Every soldier deprived of the ammunition, food, and medicine that goes down with the barge—their blood will be on his hands, too.

Soldiers like Vasily. Frontoviki desperate for the supplies being unloaded before his eyes.

Artem knows, all at once, that he is no better than the traitor Natasha. In fact, he is much worse—a filthy murderer skulking in the mud of the landing site.

He remembers the words of the commissar from that August day in Lenin Square when Stalingrad still stood proud. *This boy is all of us. This boy is Russia. And we are the motherland!*

Tears come to his eyes. He takes his trembling fingers away from the bead and lets the grenade fall, unarmed, from his hands. It hits the water with a soft *sploosh* and vanishes into the darkness. Artem stares after it. A flare pops overhead and the surface of the water becomes a mirror. Artem's face appears, backlit by the fiery glow. A motorboat's wake stirs the river. His reflection breaks into a million pieces and disappears.

CHAPTER

OCTOBER

"Welcome to my emporium, Artem Romanovich."

Fyodor Nikolaevich couldn't be more different from his imposing and elegant father, Nikolai. The elderly man carried himself with the air of the *nomenklatura*—high-ranking Party members—despite living in the same shabby building as Artem. The son, on the other hand, favors baggy suits that seem to billow from his well-built, powerful frame. His thick fingers are crowded with gaudy rings that clack together as he moves his hands. Even now, in the wreckage of Stalingrad, he sits behind a desk in the corner of a basement room like a boss overseeing his factory. His unruly black hair is coated in fine dust that shakes loose with every distant artillery barrage. The bare bulb strung overhead swings back and forth with each blast. Fyodor's fleshy face moves in and out of shadow as he gestures broadly to either side of the desk.

"We're undergoing some renovations at the moment, courtesy of the German Sixth Army."

Artem glances around. Fyodor's basement is piled high with all manner of goods. Clean linens and quilts, neatly folded. Full bars of soap. Cans of fizzy water with syrup. Woolen socks. Artem's darting gaze comes to rest on a table full of utensils: not just forks and spoons, but nutcrackers and ornate carving knives. Underneath the table is a messy stack of bicycle wheels.

"Can I interest you in a candle?" Fyodor holds up a half-melted lump of wax. He sniffs it and makes a face. "Very fragrant. Wonderful item." He sets it down on the desk and picks up a silver egg. "Paperweight? Keep your important documents in place?" He taps it on the desk. "Not today? All right, all right. Maybe tomorrow."

He leans back, puts his feet up on the desk, and produces a wet-looking cigar, which he sticks in his mouth yet does not bother to light. "What can I do for you?"

Artem takes a deep breath. His mother told him that men like Fyodor relish small talk, that he should work up to what he needs—that Fyodor might even be insulted by a hurried attitude. "First," Artem says, "I want to tell you that I'm sorry about your father."

Fyodor bows his head, chewing the end of the cigar. Then he takes it out of his mouth, glances at it with disgust, and tosses it over his shoulder. It hits the cement wall and falls to the floor. "They say you never hear the one that gets you. I heard the one that got *him*, though. Blew the whole building to smithereens." His small, sunken eyes blink on like two distant headlights. "He was a good man. But all is not lost, Artem Romanovich." He rummages in a drawer and comes up with a pocket watch. He taps the cracked face. "Twice a day it's right. And it's yours for"—he swings his feet onto the floor, leans over the top of the desk, and peers down at Artem's feet—"those boots." He throws himself back down into his chair and shakes the watch in front of Artem's face. "Well? A bargain, no?"

"No thank you," Artem says.

Fyodor shrugs and tosses the pocket watch back into the drawer. "Can't give that thing away." He sighs, shaking his head. "Men and their pocket watches. I bet Anna Olegovna has one of your father's squirreled away somewhere." He pauses, studying Artem like a jeweler inspecting a diamond. "You have his eyes, you know."

Artem has heard this before from people old enough to have known his father. "I wish I could have met him."

"Brilliant man. A bit absent-minded, head in the clouds. He was a typical scientist in many ways, but in others, well . . ." His face emerges from the shadows with a gentle smile. "He could be full of surprises. You know, he once helped me clear up a small matter with the local Party boss, a very nosy man. This was before your father fell into disfavor with them, obviously." He shakes his head. "It was a tragedy, what happened to him. My own father used to say, you should be more like Roman Andreyovich."

Something tugs at the back of Artem's mind. What Fyodor is saying doesn't make sense. "Fyodor Nikolaevich, forgive me, but . . ." Artem pauses, wondering if it's worth continuing, if he should just keep his mouth shut and move on. "If we didn't move into the building until after my father was sent away, how did you know him?"

He braces himself for a surge of anger, already berating himself for being so nosy. But to his surprise, Fyodor throws back his round head and laughs heartily. "My boy, your mother has kept you too sheltered for my liking. Ach! I have no children, what am I saying? She was just doing what's best for you, no doubt. But these old family secrets seem to matter less and less every day, don't you think?" He points to the planks and pieces of cloth that make up the rickety ceiling. A shell lands somewhere nearby. Fyodor plunks his elbows on the desk and leans forward. "Your father was a bit like me."

Artem's mind churns. "A criminal?" he blurts out.

Fyodor laughs once again. "No, no, not *that* much like me. He was a scientist through and through. But if he wanted to buy, say, a bicycle for your brother—very nice item, very rare in the stores here, very expensive—he was not above doing favors for certain people. People like me."

Artem tries to imagine his father, the scientist, skulking in some dark alley, meeting a man like Fyodor.

Fyodor watches him puzzle this out with amusement. "It is not so strange, I assure you. In this world, we all must do what we can for our piece of the pie, as the Westerners say. Only here, the pie is seldom baked, and you have to know the right people to get your piece. Anyway! I talk too much."

Artem files all this away for later. Right now, he has a job to do. The original job that Vasily assigned to him.

"My mother can't walk. Her leg isn't getting better and she has these fevers."

"Terrible," Fyodor says. "She is lucky to have you."

There's that word again, Artem thinks. *Lucky.* "She can't stay here much longer or she'll die. She forgets things all the time. Sometimes she doesn't know where she is." Before the war came to Stalingrad, this kind of talk would bring tears to his eyes. Now, he hasn't quite grown numb to the suffering, but he *has* gotten used to it. "Sometimes she talks to my father." Artem leaves out his terrible suspicion that this means his mother's soul is drifting closer to the other world, the land of the dead.

Fyodor sighs. "I know why you came to see me. I know what you're going to ask. But to evacuate someone under the noses of the Germans *and* the Russians is no easy task. And taking someone who can't walk under her own steam . . ." He shakes his head sadly.

"But it *is* possible," Artem says hopefully.

"Anything is possible for the right price," Fyodor says. "But I'm afraid it's going to cost more than an old pair of worn-out boots." He searches in his desk drawer and pulls out a cracked teacup and saucer. "Perhaps she would like this instead? Only one boot."

Artem reaches down and hefts the impossibly heavy pack. With two hands, he plops it down on the desk with a thud. Fyodor looks startled. He reaches for the canvas flap, then eyes Artem suspiciously. "This isn't going to explode, is it?"

Artem shakes his head.

"Because I will be upset. I very much like my hands and fingers."

"I promise."

Fyodor opens the pack. His eyes go wide. He reaches in and removes a stack of German army ration tins. Then another. And another.

Everything Artem managed to squirrel away from his dealings with the oberst. It had taken all his willpower not to feast on them when the hunger of the past few weeks gnawed his guts. But he knew they would be worth more to him if he managed to save them up. And now it's time to cash in.

"Well, well, Artem Romanovich. Full of surprises."

"Is that enough?"

"Yes, yes." Fyodor pushes himself up out of his chair and begins transferring the ration tins to the table with the utensils. "Enough to open up a café. Fyodor's Canned Bratwurst Palace. I'll string some festive lights from the ceiling."

"I know how we can get her out. I just need help." Artem proceeds to tell Fyodor about the evacuation of wounded soldiers at the central district's landing site. Once he gets to talking, he finds that he can't stop. All his plans, however far-fetched, come tumbling out. Disguises, stretchers, bribes for Red Army medics.

Fyodor laughs at Artem's rapid-fire ideas. "I'm starting to think you and your father are peas in a pod." He transfers the last of the ration tins to the table. "Don't worry, Artem. You've done enough worrying for one lifetime. I will take it from here. And in one week's time, Anna Olegovna will be across the river." He gives Artem a crisp army salute. "Until then, stay safe."

Fyodor hands Artem the empty pack and begins sorting the ration tins, whistling to himself. A moment later, he notices that Artem is still here. He frowns. "Is there something else?"

"There is one other thing."

Fyodor sighs. "There always is."

"I have a friend."

"That's wonderful."

"Yuna. The Germans captured her." He leaves out the part about his deal with the oberst, and his failure to blow up the ammunition barge to secure Yuna's freedom.

Fyodor raises an eyebrow. "Is she still in Stalingrad?"

"I don't know."

He takes a deep breath and lets it out. "My boy, Comrade Stalin has dictated that anyone who falls into German hands is a traitor. Now, whether or not I agree with that view is neither here nor there. But unless you know where we can get a few spare T-34 tanks and a howitzer, I think you're just going to have to let her go."

Artem takes another look around the cluttered basement. He spies Fyodor's violin in the corner, then points at a pair of binoculars resting on a serving dish. "How about those?"

Fyodor raises an eyebrow. Then he shrugs. "Sold."

CHAPTER

The oberst's command post has moved to a new German strongpoint closer to the Volga: an old repair shop at the edge of a small freight yard, fortified with the shattered sidings of train cars. Artem crouches behind the charred remnants of *something*—a workshop, a hut, an outhouse. He has no idea. Like the rest of Stalingrad, it is useless as a permanent shelter but will serve as a temporary hiding spot.

This is the Germans' great blunder—why they can push the Red Army to the banks of the Volga yet cannot take the city outright. Their bombs have created a labyrinth of trenches and shelters for machine-gun nests and snipers. Their devastating weapons might have destroyed Stalingrad, but at the same time they birthed a new city for a new kind of war. A terrible grinding battle the Germans call *Rattenkrieg*: the War of the Rats.

Artem raises the binoculars to his eyes. One of the lenses is cracked, so it's more like a single spyglass, but it does the job. He turns a dial to focus the lens on the repair shop.

Suddenly, his hand begins to tremble. The lens bounces against his eye socket, and the repair shop jumps and blurs. He tries to take control of his hand, but it's like a wire has been cut in his mind. He lowers the binoculars and stares at his palm. The tremor does not subside. It gets worse. Artem closes his eyes and takes a few deep breaths. Somewhere close by, a machine gun fires a stream of bullets that goes unanswered. Just some listless shooting. Stalingrad's constant background noise.

It takes several minutes to steady himself. Artem's very body seems entirely outside his control. Troubling, but there's nothing he can do. Right now he has more important things on his mind.

He raises the binoculars again, adjusts the dial, and sweeps the working lens across the fortified repair shop. There are German sentries behind sandbags. The familiar sight of gun barrels poking out. With the eye of a Stalingrad veteran, Artem picks out the positions of German soldiers posted across the bleak landscape. Artillery spotters roam on the roof of one semi-intact building, an apartment block only half destroyed. More than likely a sniper's nest is perched in the shadows behind the collapsed smokestack. A communication post has been dug into a hill behind the repair shop, its wires snaking across the ground.

Movement behind the rolls of razor wire that enclose the command post catches his eye. He centers it in the lens.

A woman in a German greatcoat marches haughtily from the repair shop, nodding at the soldiers she passes along the way. Artem holds his breath as he turns the dial to bring her into focus. Rouge, lipstick, hair done up stylishly.

Natasha. The traitor at the oberst's side. The woman who got Yuna captured. Artem keeps her in the lens as she saunters through the German strongpoint and descends into a trench. A moment later, a smaller figure climbs out. Fine black silt coats the lens. Artem wipes it clean with a sleeve in time to catch this new figure moving quickly through a demolished house and out the other side. In her hands is a carton. A hood is pulled tightly over her head in the October chill.

Artem draws in a breath and holds it. He can't see her face, but he knows those quick, darting movements anywhere. The upright stick bug. A moment later she disappears inside the repair shop.

He breathes out and lowers the binoculars. His hand trembles.

Yuna!

CHAPTER

Artem tilts the spout of the wineskin into his mother's mouth and squeezes out the last drop of water. He mops her brow with a dirty cloth. Despite the cold—the first hint of winter's bitterness creeping in—her face is damp with sweat. Her glazed eyes stare at nothing. Artem tosses the cloth and the wineskin aside and takes her clammy hand.

"I need to talk to you," he says. He doesn't know how much she will understand in the grip of her fever, but he doesn't want her to be afraid.

Her head turns. She looks at him in confusion. Then her hand seems to come to life, gripping his with surprising force.

"Vasily!" she exclaims. "Sit, sit. I'll put on some tea."

"No, Mom," he says slowly. "It's me—it's Artem."

Her eyes narrow. "You don't have to speak to me like I'm a hundred years old," she snaps.

"Listen. Do you remember how you told me that Fyodor Nikolaevich was alive?"

She frowns, thinking. He can see her struggle to put a face to the name. "Yes," she says at last. "I heard his violin."

"You were right. He is alive. And I went to see him. He's agreed to help us."

Her expression darkens. "For what price?"

"A fair one," Artem says. He doesn't tell her that he traded almost all their ration tins. Outside, katyusha rockets scream across the city. Distant explosions filter down into their shelter. Artem takes his mother's hand in both of his and tries to keep them from shaking. "He's going to bring you across the river, to the other side, where it's safe. They'll be able to help you there. You'll have doctors and nurses and clean sheets and a real bed. And food!" He smiles. "You're going to be okay."

An unfamiliar warmth swells in his chest. It takes him a moment to realize that it's pride. He is finally able to do what his brother asked of him—get his mother to safety. He sends a silent message to Vasily, wherever he is—*I'm doing it.*

But Anna Olegovna regards him suspiciously. Artem guiltily wishes her fever would descend like a veil over her mind, just for a little while, to make this easier. Then he pushes that thought away. He's happy she's alert.

"And what about you?" she says.

He pauses. *Well, you see, first I have to figure out how to save Yuna from the Germans . . .*

Artem still hasn't told her about Yuna's capture. And he won't break the news to her now.

"I'll be right behind you," he says. Inside, he cringes. It's a feeble lie, and it comes out that way.

With a surge of strength, his mother pulls him down toward her. "I am not leaving this place without you, Artem. I already lost a husband. And a son."

"Vasily's not *lost*," Artem protests, but he realizes how absurd this is to say. He has no idea where his brother is, or even if he's alive. That is the definition of *lost*.

There are millions of frontoviki, all of them lost to the people who love them.

"I won't lose you, too!" his mother says. She clings to his hands as if to prove that she will hold on to him forever. Artem makes a silent vow that when he joins his mother across the river, he will tell her about everything: the oberst, the canteens, the grenade, Yuna's capture. But for now, he stays quiet.

"The boy is correct! He will be right behind you." The deep voice booms into the shelter. Artem wheels around. Fyodor Nikolaevich is there, looming in the entrance. He is wearing a thick wool cap with fuzzy flaps dangling over his ears. The sight of this startles Artem—Fyodor is wearing winter clothes. It's only October, but the brutal cold is coming.

In Stalingrad, winter feels like it lasts for eight months. And if finding food is hard now, it'll be impossible when the city is frozen solid. He shakes off a sudden stab of dread.

"Nikolai Gregorovich!" his mother gasps.

Fyodor steps into the shelter, sets a canvas army pack on the dirt floor, and produces a soiled Red Army uniform and greatcoat.

He smiles sadly at his father's name. "Close enough. Now, it's time for our costume party." He shakes out the uniform like he's just pulled fresh laundry from a clothesline. Artem notices holes in the fabric, rimmed in what looks like blood. He wonders if Fyodor made the uniform look like that, or if he took it from a dead soldier.

Fyodor catches him staring. He lowers his voice. "Don't ask questions you don't want to know the answer to."

Suddenly, two women duck into the shelter, bringing with them the rank smell of combat: sweat and fear and smoke and fire. They are dressed in the gray-green of soldiers, but they carry satchels emblazoned with red cross symbols. Army field medics.

One of them goes straight to his mother, pushing Artem aside, and begins speaking to her in a low voice. She tilts a small vial into Anna Olegovna's mouth.

"Wait!" Artem says. "What's that?"

"Just something to keep her calm," the medic says.

Artem squeezes his mother's hands. "I'll see you soon," he says. "I love you."

"I love you, too," she says, smiling weakly. He can already see the drift behind her eyes as she floats away.

I hope it's somewhere nice, Artem thinks. He turns to the medic as she pockets the vial. "Take care of her. Please."

"I take care of everyone as best I can," the medic says. "Sometimes they live, sometimes they die."

Artem's mouth drops open. He is stunned by her coldness.

Fyodor lays a hand on his shoulder and speaks to him in a whisper. "All day and all night, they tend to wounded comrades. They have seen horrible things. You can forgive them for their strained bedside manner."

Artem nods. The two medics take the bloody uniform and begin to bustle around his mother.

"Wait outside," Fyodor says.

Numb, Artem obeys. Outside in the courtyard trench, it is dark and cold. He gazes out beyond the ruins of his building, across the eerie half-light that lies over the city like a shroud. It is the glow of a thousand small fires that never go out. Shell bursts and muzzle flashes. Artem climbs the ladder until his head peeks over the top of the trench. Dark piles of rubble rise from the ground like alien mushrooms. His eyes rove the emptiness. At this time of year, the courtyard has always been home to all manner of small creatures. But now the badgers, hedgehogs, and even the dogs have fled. Everything except the spiders.

"Misha!" he calls out softly. "Misha-cat!"

Silence, except for the katyusha rockets' ceaseless howl. Somewhere, a German position is getting hammered by a Red Army attack. Artem finds no joy in this—simply a dull acknowledgment that it's happening.

After a few minutes, Fyodor comes out to join him. Artem hops down off the ladder. Fyodor pulls a flask from his greatcoat and takes a deep swig.

"Your friend," he says, "who was taken by the Germans."

"She's still here," Artem says. "In the city. I saw her, way behind the lines. They're forcing her to be some kind of servant now."

"What will you do?"

"I'm going to get her back."

Fyodor sighs. "Your mother is right, you know. She has already lost so much."

A German flare pops over the landing site, several kilometers east. The glow paints dark shadows underneath Fyodor's eyes and nose. A complex feeling rises inside Artem. A need to explain things to Fyodor, because his mother is beyond understanding and he has no one else to talk to.

"When I was really little," he says, "I saw a hawk swoop down and kill a rabbit up on the Mamayev Kurgan. The hawk tore it to pieces, right in front of me. There were lots of other rabbits who lived up there, too. *Oryctolagus cuniculus.*" He pauses, feeling a little silly. But Fyodor nods, encouraging him to go on. "I thought, that rabbit was part of a family. There's a mama rabbit, brother and sister rabbits. Just because they're animals doesn't mean they love their family any less than we do, right?"

"I don't know," Fyodor says.

"At the time I was upset. My brother had to tell me all about predators and prey, and how the natural world is a giant food chain. Anyway, that got me thinking: Rabbits don't treat other rabbits like they're above them. Rabbits are all in the same place on the food chain. There aren't huge groups of rabbits preying on other rabbits. But people are all in the same place on the food chain, too. And *we* prey on other people. So what's wrong with us if the rabbits are more advanced?"

Fyodor laughs sadly. "I am but a simple criminal, Artem. This kind of philosophy is beyond me."

"I'm just saying, Hitler and the Germans think they can make themselves the predators and everybody else the prey. And if I let them send Yuna to the camps, I don't know, it's like I'm *agreeing* with them by doing nothing."

"So *rabbits* are going to be the reason you get yourself killed."

"No," Artem says, embarrassed. "Forget about the rabbits. It's because Yuna's my friend, okay? And my mother tried to save her before the Germans even got here. She knew what would happen. She would *want* me to do this."

"I think Anna Olegovna would want you to stay alive."

"I won't get killed if you help me! You found those two medics. You could get some soldiers, and we could—"

The two medics exit the shelter, bearing Artem's mother on a stretcher between them. Even in the darkness of the trench, Artem can tell that his mother has been dressed in the Red Army uniform. The medics move past him without a word. His mother lies still. He catches sight of a bloodstained hole in the uniform and for a moment the false wound seems all too real. His heart pounds.

Fyodor glances at the medics as they walk by, then tucks the flask back into his greatcoat. "I'm sorry, boy," he says. "But our transaction is finished. Anna Olegovna will be safe." He lays a heavy hand on Artem's shoulder. "Don't die for the rabbits, Artem. Don't die for your friend, either. Goodbye."

With that, Fyodor shuffles away into the darkness.

Artem waits until they're out of earshot, then he climbs the ladder once again. His gaze moves across the empty courtyard, stops at the place where he once found a long-eared hedgehog nosing around inside a fallen trash can. Now there's only a pile of scorched bricks.

For the first time in his life, he is completely alone.

First my father, he thinks. *Then my brother. Now my mother.*

He tries to take solace in the fact that he has just saved his mother's life. But the world feels much colder than it did earlier. He doesn't know if it's the early winter or the fact that he could fall off the ladder right now and crack his head open, and there would be no one to come to his aid. He thinks of the medics. How strange it is that to care for people in Stalingrad, you have to make it so you don't *really* care about anyone at all.

It's all too much for him. He takes a deep breath. Then he calls out in a low voice.

"Misha! Misha-cat!"

He listens. There is only the chatter of a machine gun, a few muffled shouts.

He tries again. This time, boldness surges. He decides he doesn't care if there's a German patrol nearby.

"Misha!" he shouts. His voice cracks sharply against the rubble, bounces around the wreckage. "Misha!" he shouts again, louder now.

Then he begins to whistle a few bars of "The Little Blue Shawl." He feels a reckless defiance grow within him. Let the Germans hear. Let them know there are still Russians in these ruins. He doesn't care. Let them come hunt their prey.

"Misha!" he screams. In his head, other cries echo. *Vasily! Mom! Yuna!*

His eyes fill with tears, but at least his hands are steady on the cold rungs of the ladder. He climbs up over the top and picks his way through the rubble, screaming for his cat. An exchange of gunfire rattles and sputters out. It's so close he can hear the bullets hitting cement.

"Misha!"

There's movement in the corner of his eye. He whirls around, fists clenched, expecting to be greeted by the barrel of a gun.

Instead, a darting blur races out of the darkness. Like a torpedo launched at a submarine, it heads straight for him. Artem can't believe his eyes.

A moment later, his spotted cat is giving his ankles fierce nudges and nose bops.

Artem scoops Misha up in his arms. Right away he can tell that the cat is very thin—he can feel the little cat bones in his spine and ribs. Holding Misha snugly against his chest, he races for the ladder.

Inside the shelter, under the dim light of the oil lamp, he places Misha on the desk. He laughs at the cat's half mustache just below his nose—it's the funniest thing he's ever seen. Misha is alive! He pokes and prods the cat all over, examining for wounds. Beyond some mangy, matted fur, the cat seems fine.

"Where have you been, kitty?" He opens the one remaining ration tin and dumps the slop out on the desk. Misha plows into the food and begins to feast. “There we go. Delicious dinner.”

Artem watches Misha eat, listening to his little cat noises as his tongue laps up the food.

“Slow down!” he says. To his great delight, the cat looks up at him with gray bits of food stuck to his nose. Then he dips his head and goes back to feasting. Artem glances over at his mother’s empty mattress, listening to his cat scarf up an entire German ration. He wonders how long it will take the medics to reach the landing site. Will they be able to get his mother on a ship? Will the ship make it across, or will it be struck by German shells? The water is already freezing, what if his mother—

Stop! he commands his whirling mind. There is no use dwelling on these things. He scratches the top of Misha’s head and turns his thoughts to Yuna.

CHAPTER

Rattenkrieg.

War of the Rats.

Artem spies one of the fat little rodents with his binoculars as it emerges from beneath the barbed wire at the edge of the German strongpoint. Another one pops out of the wreckage and races after it. These rats are the same color as the sky on this dismal afternoon.

Rain comes down. The afternoon wears on. Water drips off the brim of his sodden forage cap. Artem's waterlogged coat clings to him like dead weight. Hunger is a knot in his stomach that is somehow both burning and cold.

Artem doesn't move. He watches the rats. With the countless beautiful and intriguing animals that live in Stalingrad, from the Mamayev Kurgan to the river, Artem has never before paid much attention to rats. Occasionally Misha would kill one and leave it as a gift in the doorway of his bedroom. He used to see them scrambling through gutters, disappearing into sewer grates.

Today he is profoundly grateful for the rats of Stalingrad.

If the Germans have turned the city into rubble and craters for the Red Army to use against them, the rats have adapted in even sneakier ways. As he watches the traffic on the little rat boulevard, Artem imagines a map overlaying the city: countless zigzagging lines sliced into the surface, the mad grid of the rat runs.

He shifts the binoculars and turns the dial. He sweeps the lens across the path between the fortified repair shop—the oberst's headquarters—and the ruins beyond. There are trenches there he can't see, he knows. Bunkers dug into the ground. Basements covered in planks and bricks. Yuna is being kept in one of them.

As the afternoon slides into darkness, Natasha emerges from the ground. Up she comes, wrapped in an absurd fur coat the Germans must have looted from a fancy house. A German soldier rushes over and opens an umbrella above her head. He walks beside her as she heads for the repair shop. A moment later, Yuna appears. No one comes to her with an umbrella. The soldiers ignore her, except for one or two who pause to jeer at her. He turns the dial and she comes into focus.

There is a yellow star sewn into her thin coat. She is carrying a green bottle. One of the passing soldiers sticks his leg out. Yuna trips. The bottle hits the ground and smashes. Natasha turns, puts her hands on her hips, and screams at Yuna. Her voice carries. Artem catches stray Russian curses.

Yuna pushes herself to her feet. Covered in mud, she trudges back to the hole in the trench and disappears.

Artem's heart aches. She must feel completely abandoned. She would have no idea he's out here, watching.

Just a little while longer, Yuna.

He sweeps the binoculars back across the blasted landscape, tracing the edge of the trench as it curls into a rat run that vanishes at the barbed wire. He waits. He tracks the rats. He watches for what feels like forever. Eventually, he sees it. The glint of metal, even in the dull evening light. A circular outline coming up from the ground beyond the wire.

A sewer tunnel, exposed by bombing and shelling and fire.

Artem waits for night to come, growing ever more soaked, watching the rats come and go. He thinks of the boy he was in August, who could barely focus on his task long enough to help Yuna fortify the fuel tanks.

Well, he thinks, *it's easy to focus now.* There's nothing to distract him. The only wild animals left in Stalingrad are the rats.

Night does not fall so much as seep out of every shell hole and trench. As darkness takes over, Artem watches the German position. Squads form to go on patrol. Others come back to rest. Shifts change at the machine-gun nests beside the repair shop.

Eventually the patrols are dispatched, and the German soldiers settle uneasily behind their defenses. Artem moves quickly and quietly from his hiding place. Staying low, he joins the rats.

CHAPTER

The tunnel has been cut off from Stalingrad's sewer system and has not been used in several weeks. Still, the stench is unbearable. Artem tilts his head and pulls up his collar so that his nose and mouth are buried in his greatcoat. The coat doesn't exactly smell like roses, either, but it's better than a sewer.

The darkness is total. The only sound is the squelching of his boots in the muck. He recalls how Fyodor Nikolaevich wanted to trade various items for these boots. Artem finds himself thankful he didn't agree.

His foot comes down on something soft and squishy. A rat squeaks and runs off.

Shards of yellow light appear up ahead. In a moment, he comes to the end of the tunnel, now boarded up with planks. The light is from a lantern on the other side, shining through gaps in the wood. Gaps just large enough for rats to squeeze through, but impossible for a human.

His heart sinks. Of course—the Germans aren't idiots. The oberst wouldn't leave an open tunnel leading straight into his headquarters.

Artem peers through one of the gaps. Beyond the walled-off section is a narrow trench, a rat run used by the Germans to crisscross their position. Stacked crates are covered with tarpaulins and blankets. There is precious little room to move between them. At the other end of the trench is a lantern dangling from a plank sticking out of the dirt wall. Two German soldiers a few years older than Vasily stand at ease beside it, chatting in low tones. Their rifles lean against the wall. Each weapon has a scope attached to the barrel. *Snipers,* Artem thinks. He breathes softly into his coat as he watches them. He wonders how many Russians they've picked off from their hiding places. *Predators and prey.*

The soldiers pick up their guns and vanish around the bend. Their voices fade away. Artem waits for a full minute, listening. Then he works his cold fingers into a gap between the planks and manages to wiggle it loose. The gap widens. It gives a little more—then stops. Try as he might, he can't open it any wider than his wrist. He slides his hand down and feels around blindly. Bricks: The floor of the trench is piled with them to hold the slats in place. Cautiously, he curls his hand around one and tosses it away from the pile. It hits the dirt floor of the trench with a dull thud.

Three more tossed bricks and Artem is able to slide the slats apart wide enough to squeeze through. He sidles down the narrow space between the crates. The rain is a light mist that seems to hang in the glow from the lantern on the wall. His eyes catch Russian words printed on the crates. He pauses, thinking. These aren't German supplies. They have been looted from his fellow citizens. He slides a corner of the tarp back and lifts the lid of a crate. Inside, vodka bottles are lined up neatly, nested in straw to keep them from breaking.

Without any kind of real plan, Artem grabs a bottle, pops the cork, and dumps its contents all over the crates. Quickly, he does it again with a second bottle. The fumes from the alcohol make his head swim. He pops a third cork and soaks as many crates as he can. Then he opens a fourth bottle and lets it dribble out as he moves through the trench. He stops where the corridor turns sharply to the left and peers around the corner. There is a ladder about five meters away. He pours out the rest of the liquid, then takes a matchbook from his pocket.

Voices drift down the trench. The two snipers, on their way back! The second they spot him, he's dead.

He strikes a match. Nothing happens. Not even a spark.

The matches are wet. In desperation he tries another. Nothing. He tosses the useless matchbook aside and rushes to the lantern. He unhooks it from the hole drilled in the plank that juts out from the wall.

The voices are louder now. He can hear footsteps, too. Heavy boots coming his way.

Artem raises the lantern above his head and throws it as hard as he can into the dirt, aiming for the dark pool where he emptied the bottle. The lantern shatters. The approaching Germans shout in alarm.

A tongue of flame unfurls from the smashed lamp. A split second later, fire is licking the crates. The first one catches with a low roar. Heat blasts Artem's face. He turns to head for the ladder—and realizes his mistake. The two snipers are rushing through the trench, coming straight at him, and the ladder is behind them.

There's no way to get there without running right through them. One of the snipers points at Artem. The other raises his rifle. Artem retreats around the bend as the bullet thunks into the wall. Now he is trapped next to the burning crates.

The misty rain is no match for the fire. Hot wind scorches his face.

The planks that once hid the entrance to the sewer tunnel are ablaze.

The snipers will round the bend in a few seconds, and then Artem is finished.

There's nowhere to go but up.

Artem plunges into the flames and leaps up onto a fallen crate. The heat lashes his skin. Smoke burns the back of his throat. But mercifully, his clothes are soaked. Tucking his hands inside the wet sleeves, he climbs onto a burning stack of crates and scrambles up over the lip of the trench. He pulls himself along, belly to the wet ground, moving through the mud and away from the blaze.

Rattenkrieg.

War of the Rats.

He is one of them now.

The fire has attracted the attention of the entire German position. They don't know if it's a Russian attack, sabotage, or some kind of accident. Men rush toward the trench from all directions, some of them barely missing Artem as he stays pressed flat to the ground in the dark. He fights the urge to close his eyes as if that will make him magically invisible instead of leaving him vulnerable.

He slithers away from the glow. The conditions of Stalingrad are in his favor now—lights draws the enemy, so the darkness is total. He slithers up out of the muck to crouch behind a pile of concrete, gazing across the trench to the place where Yuna had emerged with the bottle.

The Germans form a line to pass buckets toward the blaze. The first man in line pours water down into the trench. Soldiers come rushing up to form a second line. At this rate, the fire will be out in a minute or two.

Artem tries to move from his hiding place and is puzzled to find that his legs will not obey. His hand begins to tremble. Again, he wills himself out from behind the rubble. *Go, Artem.*

Forcing himself up is like trying to use his shoulder to push through a brick wall. In his mind, the sniper's bullet whistles past his head, again and again. *Thunk. Thunk. Thunk.*

The second he raises his head it could be blown off. The Germans might know exactly where the dumb Russian kid is who just climbed out of their trench. Fyodor's words echo in his mind. *Don't die for your friend.*

He slides his hands under his armpits and squeezes them tightly against the sides of his chest to steady them. He pushes all the voices out and lands on a single memory: Yuna dangling the feather toy for Misha to swipe at. Misha who is back in the shelter now. Waiting for his new friend to come home.

That does it. Artem's legs finally obey him. He moves through wreckage toward the dark slit of the trench's eastern edge. At the other end, the soldiers work to put out the fire, bathed in orange light. Artem is alone. He peers over the rim. There is a lantern hanging from a plank. On either side of the lantern, blankets cover bunkers dug into the main trench. Artem's eyes rove until he sees a ladder. He moves along the edge of the trench, staying low, then climbs down. He tries not to think about the German sentries that could come around a corner at any moment.

He comes to the first blanket and grips it in his fist. There might be a gun barrel waiting for him on the other side. He listens. Silence. His heart races. He throws the blanket aside. Stale air wafts out. His eyes pick out dim forms in the lamplight. A small army cot. A few books. A sheathed knife hanging on a peg. Other than that, it's empty.

He moves to the next bunker. His nerve endings feel exposed. He is an infection in the enemy's veins, surrounded by their killer white blood cells. He pulls the blanket aside—

—and instantly his vision explodes into a bright web of starlight. Dull pain thuds between his ears. Time jumps forward and he finds that he's on the floor of the trench. He feels sick. His ears ring. A figure looms over him. He looks up, waiting for the next blow, or the final shot. He blinks.

"Yuna?" he croaks.

She is standing over him, clutching a green bottle by the neck. There is her filthy coat with the yellow star pinned to her chest. Her face is smudged with dirt. Her eyes are wild, fierce—*vicious.* They go wide with recognition.

"Artem?"

He rubs the side of his head where the bottle connected with his skull. "Ow."

The bottle hits the dirt. Yuna reaches down and helps him up. His vision blurs. Her face wavers in front of him, and when she speaks her voice is far away.

"I thought you were one of them!"

Artem forces his eyes to focus. "I'm me."

Yuna throws her arms around him. "How did you get in here?"

"Later," he says, staggering toward the ladder. "No time." The trench walls tilt crazily. His shoulder bumps a plank. The black sky is everywhere. Yuna grabs hold of his arms to keep him from falling.

"Artem! They'll shoot us."

He shakes his head. "Fire."

"What?"

"I made a fire."

They reach the ladder at the same time. Yuna goes first. She pauses at the top and raises her head carefully over the partition. Artem watches her head turn. Back and forth, back and forth, a pale little blob against the black sky. He rubs his eyes.

"Come on!" she hisses.

He climbs up. Together, they hit the dirt just beyond the trench and make for the shadows. Artem looks to the east. The orange glow makes his heart leap. "It's still going!" he says. The soldiers' bucket brigade is still passing water along its assembly line. He gives her a triumphant grin. "I found an old sewer tunnel under the fence. The rats showed me."

"Wow, I guess I hit you pretty hard. So where is this sewer tunnel?"

He points to the blazing trench. "There!"

"You set our escape route on fire?"

His grin disappears. "I didn't think about that."

"It's okay." She gazes off into the distance, then turns back to Artem. "Follow me."

CHAPTER

So what were you going to do if it wasn't me back there?" Artem asks. They are hiding on the western edge of the German strongpoint, in the remnants of a workers' hut. One wall has been reduced to a pile of brick and timber, but the other three stand high enough to hide them from view.

"The same thing I *did* do," Yuna says. While Artem slouches against the wall, holding his throbbing head in his hands, Yuna can barely contain her energy. She moves from place to place, peering out into the darkness.

"You were going to smash a German soldier over the head? Then what?"

"Run. Tomorrow they were putting me on a train to a camp." She pauses. "So I had nothing to lose, right? If they shot me here, it would have been better than freezing to death out there. Or worse. Anyway, at least if I ran, I'd have a tiny chance of making it back to you and Anna."

A surge of warmth begins in Artem's chest. It moves out into his limbs until his fingers and toes tingle. He watches Yuna as she puts her hands on her hips and leans toward a jagged gap in the wall.

"I sent my mother across the river," Artem tells her. He knows he should be happy about this—they both should—but he finds that he is a little nervous to break the news to Yuna. She turns away from the wall.

"You did?" Then she smiles. "Artem, that's great! How did you manage that?"

"I had to trade our ration tins." He is on the verge of telling her about Misha's return, too, but decides to keep it a surprise.

"I know how we can get more food," Yuna says.

"Really? How?"

She bends back to the hole in the wall. "Come on. We need to move."

She leads him out of the hut. He glances off to where the glow from the fire has grown dim. The soldiers are dispersing back through the darkness toward the repair shop, where the torn sides of freight cars jut up into the night. Yuna leads him behind a twisted sculpture of metal and points to one of the machine-gun nests alongside the shop. Artem can just barely make out the helmet of the soldier behind the sandbags.

Yuna points into the darkness. "I've brought the oberst food and champagne enough times to see that there's a little gap between the guard post and the repair shop."

"I can't see it."

"It's really small."

"Can we fit through it?"

"I think so."

"You *think*?"

"Well, well!" At the sound of the Russian voice, Artem is gripped by a chill. He turns to find Natasha emerging from the darkness, wrapped in her fur coat, a bottle hanging loosely from her fingers. "You know, Yuna, you might not think so, but I am your best friend." She gestures around. "Where else are you going to go? There is barely any city anymore, and the Germans own what's left. This is the safest place for us." She looks toward the repair shop. *"Hans!"* she yells out. *"Your Jew is escaping!"*

Without a word, Artem and Yuna sprint toward the guard post. Natasha giggles behind them. "Run, fools, run!"

Out of the corner of his eye, Artem catches sight of the oberst as the German officer exits his headquarters, flanked by a pair of soldiers. "There!" he yells, spotting Artem and Yuna immediately, even in the dark.

Shots ring out. Artem wishes he'd set the repair shop on fire instead. He wishes he'd kept the German grenade rather than dumping it into the Volga. He wishes—

A hot jolt of pain sears the back of his upper arm. *I've been shot,* he thinks. But his legs are still carrying him toward the guard post.

More shots plink off the armored sides of the repair shop.

"In here!" Yuna calls out, one step ahead of him as she dives for the sandbags at the edge of the guard post and vanishes from sight. Artem has no idea where he's going, but there is nothing else to do but launch himself after her. The sentry manning the machine gun leans over the side of the sandbags. He screams in German as his arm comes down. Artem twists out of the way as he dives. The blade of a trench knife buries itself in a sandbag, inches from his side. Artem scrambles after Yuna through a tiny opening made by the edge of the sandbags and a piece of metal that curls inward, toward the repair shop.

The sentry ducks as shots from his fellow soldiers thud into the sandbags. The oberst screams out a command. Artem wriggles through the mud, jagged metal pulling at the fabric of his coat.

The moment they emerge from the mouth of the German strongpoint, the machine guns open up. Bright hyphens of tracer bullets slice through the night. Artem leads Yuna in a mad zigzagging run through the ruins. He knows this district well—it's where he has been hiding to watch the rats. Together they scramble away until the guns lose track of them in the maze of rubble. Eventually, the firing stops. Breathing hard, Artem and Yuna sit with their backs to the wall of what used to be a kitchen. A porcelain sink lies across a splintered chair.

Gingerly, Artem reaches around his upper arm and places a fingertip against the wound there. He winces at a jolt of pain.

"Are you hit?" Yuna asks.

He moves his arm. "I think it just grazed me. Are *you* hit?"

She wiggles her fingers and moves her legs. "I don't think so."

Soaked in adrenaline, Artem can barely sit still. Images flash through his mind: the sewer tunnel, the fire, the snipers in the trench, Natasha, the oberst, the guns . . .

He closes his eyes and says a silent *thank-you* to the rats who showed him the way.

"I can't believe you did that," Yuna says. Artem opens his eyes and looks at her. "I remember when you could barely handle shoveling some dirt!" She laughs. "I used to get so mad. Oh, Artem." She leans over and hugs him gently. His arm throbs—so does his head—but he doesn't protest. "Thank you. You and Anna Olegovna—without you, I'd be dead."

She rips the yellow star from her coat and tosses it away. "Or worse."

Artem doesn't ask what she means by that. He knows what awaited her in the camps.

The same fate could befall them here, too. "We need to find food," Artem says. "I know where we can get some horsemeat." He thinks of the fires and the cauldrons he has seen cropping up around his neighborhood.

"I've got a better idea," Yuna says. "I spent enough time in the oberst's headquarters, serving him and his officers, that eventually they forgot this girl pouring their drinks and cleaning their dishes was even there. So I heard them talk. Any day now, the Germans are going to put all their strength into attacking the factories in the northern part of the city: the tractor works, the Barrikady, and the Red October plants. I even saw a map, so I know exactly how it's going to work. The German Sixth Army will push the Fifty-First Guards Rifle Division out of the factories and into the Volga. If we can get to General Chuikov, we can trade our information for food!" She pauses. "Maybe he'll even send us across the river, out of the city!"

Artem barely hears this last part. His entire body, still pulsing with adrenaline, has suddenly gone cold.

"Did you say the Fifty-First is defending the factories?"

"Yes. Definitely. I memorized everything."

Artem's mouth goes dry. Hundreds of thousands of Germans and their tanks, bringing fire and death to the defenders of the factory complex. He looks at Yuna in horror. "That's my brother's division!"

CHAPTER

NOVEMBER

"If it isn't the veterinarian, Artem Romanovich Sokolov!"

The commissar greets him with glee. Artem blinks, astonished—the man standing before him in the low-ceilinged bunker is the same bright-eyed political officer who whipped the crowd into a frenzy in Lenin Square back in August. Before Artem received his city defense assignment. Before he ever met Yuna. Before the first German bombs dropped. Before, before, before . . .

"How strange," the commissar continues, "that the twists and turns of outrageous fortune have brought us to this moment! If Comrade Stalin hadn't rightly purged our nation of its treacherous priesthood, I might be inclined to tilt my head toward a holy man in an effort to understand the mystical forces behind such a divine meeting."

The bunker is small and cluttered. Maps lie across a rough-hewn table, their corners held down with shell casings. A pair of lanterns cast an eerie glow. Artem isn't sure what he had been expecting of a general's headquarters. Something grander, perhaps. But that's silly, he reminds himself. It has taken them a week to even locate the headquarters, since it's constantly moving after being destroyed several times by German artillery.

A week spent surviving on scraps of rancid horse flesh.

A week spent cowering under a torrent of bombs and artillery.

A week spent skulking through the Red Army positions dug into the cliffs by the river, getting turned away from checkpoint after checkpoint.

"It's good to see you again, comrade commissar," Artem forces himself to say. "I can't believe you remember me from that day in the square."

"I remember everything. And everyone." The eager gleam in the commissar's eye has not been dimmed by months of war. The man is clean-shaven, his uniform crisp and pressed. Meanwhile, Artem is conscious of the filth caked on his face, the rank odor of his coat, the rumbling of his empty stomach. "This is Yuna," he says, introducing the commissar to the equally dirty girl at his side.

The commissar eyes her curiously. "The general's adjutant tells me you were recently a guest of the Germans."

"Not a guest," Yuna says, her voice laced with bitterness.

Artem's nerves are frayed. Stalin has decreed that Russians taken prisoner by the Germans are to be viewed as traitors. Everyone knows that Stalin's own son was taken prisoner and Stalin refused to bargain for his release. And political officers like the commissar are extensions of Stalin's will on the battlefield.

"We have information!" Artem says, before the commissar digs into the story of Yuna's captivity and escape. "Important intelligence about—"

There is a sudden rustling movement from inside the front of his greatcoat. The commissar looks puzzled. Misha pops his head up through Artem's collar and looks around the bunker. Then he meows once in irritation.

"And who is this little comrade?" the commissar says.

"Misha," Artem says, gently pushing the cat's head back down inside the coat.

"You take him around the city with you?"

"He was lost once. I don't want to lose him again."

"We have important intelligence about a German attack!" Yuna says impatiently.

Misha shuffles around, disturbing the lice that have taken refuge beneath the fabric of Artem's threadbare shirt. Artem shifts his weight and tries not to scratch. The commissar watches him.

"You know," the officer says, "if you bury your clothes and leave a little corner showing, the lice will crawl up to the exposed point and you can burn them away. Our babushkas are sometimes smarter than all the scientists in Moscow."

"The Sixth Army is going to attack the factories, comrade commissar!" Yuna practically shouts. The commissar turns to her. "It's going to be their final assault. They're throwing everything they have at us. Panzer tanks, Stukas, hundreds of thousands of troops. I can draw their plans on a map. I've heard their officers talk about them. I've *seen* them. We've been trying to tell all this to General Chuikov for a week now."

"The general is out," the commissar says. "He is very busy, as you might imagine. However, I am his political officer. Any tactical information you have for him should be given to me."

Yuna looks at Artem. Ignoring his fear that this has already gone very wrong, Artem gives her a little nod. He wishes the general were here. Chuikov is supposed to be a reasonable man. He'd rather be speaking to anyone but this bright-eyed commissar.

"Please," Yuna says. "We need food."

The commissar looks at her quizzically. "What does that have to do with your information about German troop movements?"

"We're starving," Artem says. He can't choke down another stringy piece of half-cooked horsemeat. And he is afraid that even the choicest bits are going to make Misha sick.

"We are *all* starving," the commissar says. Artem nearly blurts out that the man looks perfectly well-fed, but manages to keep his mouth shut. "Our frontoviki have their rations cut every week, and their ammunition is running out. The Volga is only half frozen, and we can't get supply ships through the grinding ice. What do you think our soldiers are doing in these kinds of conditions?"

Artem and Yuna don't say anything. Artem's heart sinks. His stomach is a hollow knot. There won't be any food for them here after all. It will be back to the streets and the horsemeat. Eventually, the people of Stalingrad will run out of dead horses.

"Our soldiers are *fighting,*" the commissar says, answering his own question. "They aren't bargaining with their superiors. They are doing their part for the motherland without complaint." His tone isn't angry or cruel. It's more like a teacher patiently lecturing a student. "Tell me. Did you learn this kind of *transactional* arrangement with your German friends?"

"They're not our friends!" Yuna practically shouts.

"Did they give you little ration tins of bratwurst and sauerkraut and cabbage in exchange for your services? I'd be very interested to know what those services consisted of."

Artem's entire body tingles with nervous energy. He thinks of the bags full of canteens.

The hand grenade he almost launched at a Red Army barge.

He feels like the commissar's piercing gaze can see right through him, into his mind. Into his heart.

The commissar smiles. "Never mind all that. You don't have to say a word." He puts a finger to his lips, then beckons them closer. Artem glances over his shoulder, half expecting an execution squad to burst into the bunker, weapons drawn. They each take a small step forward. The commissar lowers his voice. "I know you were just doing what you had to do to survive. Despite what he says publicly for the sake of the motherland, I can assure you Comrade Stalin understands your plight, and the impossible decisions you have been forced to make. That is why, in his wisdom, he has allowed for the creation of the *shtrafroty*—special Red Army companies for deserters, cowards, traitors, and people like you, who might have engaged in some, shall we say, *questionable* behavior." The commissar is beaming. "Instead of executing you and throwing your lives away, you will be given the chance for redemption. Through hard work and sacrifice, you can prove your worth to the motherland, despite everything you've done." He looks from Artem to Yuna. "Is that satisfactory?"

Not like we have a choice, Artem thinks.

"Yes," Yuna says softly.

"Wonderful!" He reaches into a box on the desk and tosses them each a Red Army ration tin. Artem looks at it. Pork stew. His stomach growls. "Eat up," the commissar says. "We leave at once."

We? Artem thinks.

"Where are we going?" Yuna asks.

"The factories, of course. Haven't you heard? The Germans are attacking, and we must all do our part to defend the motherland."

CHAPTER

The Stalingrad tractor works rises in great, confounding slabs of steel and concrete. Artem is awed by the majesty of the factory's ruin. His life since August has been defined by a city reduced to low heaps of slag. But even half destroyed, the factories hold on to their height. Chimneys and smokestacks rise, full of holes from German shells. Heaps of steel girders and twisted metal sparkle with a coating of coal dust. Fields of broken freight cars and abandoned tanks stretch the length of city blocks. Repair shops loom, dark canopies of half-vaulted ceilings like the bones of some ancient beast, collapsing into the Russian dirt. Fires burn in ravines like blazing arrows pointed straight from the factories to the river. It is a new kind of hell within the boundaries of the old one.

"Here come the screamers!" a soldier calls out.

Artem peeks out of the fortified basement and watches the skies to the south. Stukas dive toward the Barrikady factory, their sirens shrieking. He turns his back on the bombs as they fall. The explosions shake the earth. Misha claws his chest. Artem's hand trembles. He slips it inside his greatcoat so Yuna won't see.

She joins him in the entrance to the basement, where a cement staircase has been torn nearly in two by some kind of violence. *Bomb or grenade,* Artem thinks. *Take your pick.* Yuna is pressed against him in the cramped space as she cranes her neck to watch the Stukas pull up out of their dives, silver birds threading dark bursts of flak.

"We could still run," Artem says quietly. The commissar is making his rounds, fanning out through the factory complex with his fellow political officers. He carries with him what he calls an Agitcult case, a small suitcase crammed with books, games, shaving kits, and a mirror. He says he is responsible for the "mental and physical well-being" of the frontoviki. Artem doesn't think a quick game of checkers would be much comfort in the face of advancing German tanks, but what does he know? He's not a soldier. Not like Vasily—who is here, somewhere, with the Fifty-First.

If he's still alive.

Artem pushes that thought away.

"And go where?" Yuna says quietly. Each word sends out a puff of steam. Winter has come to Stalingrad. "The river is half frozen, remember? Nothing's moving. Even if we could find a way to get across, we'd have to wait until it freezes over completely."

A blast of icy wind curls down the ruined stairs, bringing with it the smell of cold iron. Artem and Yuna step back into the basement. Down here, with the factory overhead, sounds are muffled and strange. Bombs are distant thuds while voices sometimes come through loud and clear. Artem has the peculiar sensation that the voices are dead soldiers' last words, doomed to bounce around fallen towers of steel.

"I know," Artem says. He imagines great ice floes on the Volga, shifting and crunching and mashing up ships like a giant's teeth.

"At least we have real food here," Yuna says, offering him a bite from her pork stew tin.

"Beats horsemeat," Artem agrees. Disembodied voices float down into the basement. He strains, listening for his brother. Vasily could be anywhere in the factory complex, which means there is a chance he's stationed nearby. A slim chance, maybe, but Artem holds on to hope like it's a magical amulet that will conjure up things as they were, put *home* back together for him and everyone else. He closes his eyes and imagines the Germans speeding backward across the empty steppe, villages and fields becoming unburnt in their wake, a million young Russians springing from their graves . . .

"It's a beautiful day in Stalingrad!" Artem's heart sinks as the commissar clomps heavily into the basement. The officer tosses a pair of gloves to Artem and another to Yuna. "Courtesy of Colonel Burev. I told him I had two new recruits who require the warmest hands for their task."

Artem pets Misha through his coat. "What task, comrade commissar?"

The commissar sets his Agitcult case down on a pile of cinder blocks. He looks like he's about to answer when he's interrupted by the sound of footsteps on the stairs. Artem moves to the back of the basement as soldiers stream wearily into the shelter, stamping the cold, wet muck from their boots as they set down their rifles and heavy packs.

This company—part of the 138th Rifle Division—began their defense of the factories with two hundred men. Now, six of them remain alive. Artem wonders if Vasily's division has been similarly depleted. He has begged these men for news of his brother, but this is not the Fifty-First, and they don't know him.

Now, these six survivors open tins and pass bottles between them. One, a fastidious sapper named Krymov, daintily presses a small scrap of a clean towel against his forehead and cheeks. Then he folds the towel and places it in a small wooden case he keeps in a pocket.

"Where's our mascot?" calls out a man they call "Chef" for reasons unknown to Artem. He has never seen Chef prepare any food.

Artem glances toward the doorway. Yuna places a board over the lower half of the entrance. Only then does Artem kneel and open the top of his coat so that Misha can hop out.

The soldiers clap solemnly as if they are at an orchestra concert as Misha rushes across the cracked floor to lap at a bowl of water. They all watch when Misha bounds up into Krymov's lap and bops his nose against the man's hand.

"To the fiercest fighter in Stalingrad!" Krymov says. The men lift their tins and bottles in salute. Misha curls up into a ball, then uncurls a second later and swipes a paw at a button on Krymov's greatcoat.

"All right, all right," the commissar says. The men take their seats against the wall. Artem studies them. Gaunt and hard-featured, they watch the commissar with a sort of wary, grudging respect. Gaining the favor of such a high-ranking party member will mean better jobs for any man who survives this battle.

"I know you're wondering why I pay special attention to you men. Some of you may feel like it's unfair—like your stern father is here to keep an eye on you. I assure you, I am not here to write reports about loosened collars or untucked uniforms. If I may speak frankly, I am here because you are heroes. And right now, the Russian people *need* heroes."

The commissar pauses to wait for the thunder of an artillery barrage to die away. It's impossible to tell if the shelling comes from the Germans or the Russians. In some places, the two armies are dug in only a few meters from each other. Thousands of men have perished in onslaughts from their own gun batteries.

The commissar puts his hands behind his back and moves about the cramped basement. It seems like it would be impossible to take two steps in any direction, yet the political officer manages to pace like a teacher in a classroom as he looks at each of the men in turn.

"I am writing a series of articles for *Red Star*." He holds up a copy of the army newspaper. "Profiles of the defenders of the tractor works, the Barrikady, the Red October. A chance for some of you to become the next Zaitsev, an inspiration for your comrades and for the people back home."

Artem glances at Yuna. They both recognize the name. Zaitsev is the most famous sniper in the Red Army. The articles about his exploits are everywhere. They say he has killed more than two hundred Germans, all by himself. The soldiers give a silent toast to Zaitsev, who is more legend than human being, and the commissar waits until each man has taken a drink.

"True communist endurance in the face of the fascist beast. And at the same time, a story of the individual's contribution to the struggle. Perhaps even a story that pushes the boundaries of what our censors will allow!" The commissar waits for this bit of mischief to sink in. The men stare back placidly, but Artem detects a shift in the energy of the basement. Maybe this commissar is really here for the well-being of the soldiers, and not to impose the iron will of the state. "A story of heroism for your mothers and sisters—for *all* the mothers and sisters back home in Moscow and Minsk. A story the entire motherland can rally behind as they have rallied behind Stalingrad itself. Do you know that this city is on the lips of the British and the Americans? That Churchill himself has praised your spirit? And after I'm through with this"—he holds up the paper and gives it a shake—"your very *names* will be known from New York to London."

"Why us, comrade commissar?" Krymov asks, scratching Misha's belly.

"And why now?" Chef asks.

The commissar grins. "Because you men are the lynchpin of Operation Uranus." He lets the words sink in. "The Germans think they can break our spirit. They think they can bring so much firepower to these factories that we will collapse and the city will finally belong to them. Hitler will throw his army against our defenses until it is bled dry. That is what we are counting on. As you keep them occupied here, General Chuikov is outflanking the entire German Sixth Army out on the steppe and herding them toward the city. Stalingrad itself is the bait in the trap. Because of your efforts here, we will encircle the Germans completely. The besiegers will become the besieged. We will starve them as they have starved us. And Stalingrad will be the grave of every last German!"

The commissar finishes on a rousing note. He looks around the basement, smiling, eyes gleaming, clearly expecting the men to leap to their feet in cheers and applause. But the soldiers barely meet one another's eyes. Krymov places Misha down onto the floor and Artem scoops him up. Chef removes a thick sock to examine his gnarled, blackened toe nails. The others pass their bottles silently between them. An atmosphere of quiet gloom descends.

"So we're the bait in a trap," Artem says. He hadn't even meant to say it out loud, not really. But he finds that he cares less for the rules of society these days. A steady diet of horsemeat and melted ice will do that. Krymov glances up with interest. Chef nudges the soldier at his side. The men wait for the commissar to confirm what they know to be true. They are to be sacrificed so that Operation Uranus can succeed.

The commissar wheels around with a fierce cast to his face. “Not you.”

His eyes dart from Artem to Yuna. “I’ve got something special in mind for the two of you.”

CHAPTER

Artem thinks of those cranes that long ago fled the city. The balconies on Lenin Square are gone, too, along with the beautiful white buildings. Even the square no longer exists, as cratered and empty as some bleak lunar surface.

His mind drifts back to that August afternoon. The sun hot on his face. Vasily's hands lifting him up.

"Boy!" the commissar's voice intrudes. The dream of sun is ripped away. A frigid wind howls against his chapped face. The ruined city stretches away beneath his feet, gray piles of concrete and steel vanishing in a haze of ash and smoke. They are huddled together behind a mess of brick that used to be a wall, in the shadows of a collapsed room that used to be an office high above the factory floor.

"Artem Romanovich!"

Gaps between the girders beneath their feet offer glimpses of the earth far below, the wrecked machinery and the bodies of the unburied dead, frozen in their final poses. One misstep and Artem and Yuna will join them, their own bodies broken by the fall.

The cranes flash through his mind, swooping down from the balconies. His heart swells with envy. Birds don't fear a long plunge, they just pull out of their dive like a Stuka—

Yuna elbows him in the side. Artem almost laughs out loud—his fear and nerves making a serious situation absurdly funny. Here he is again in his own little world, thinking about some animal!

The commissar thrusts a heavy satchel into Artem's gut. The force of it nearly doubles him over. "This is yours now."

Artem sets the satchel down and Yuna pulls back the flap. Inside is a clunky metal box full of dials. Wires snake along its surface, along with words in a foreign language. It's not German. Artem thinks it might be English.

"A wireless radio, courtesy of the Americans," the commissar explains. "From now on, you will never be separated from it. This radio is as vital to your survival as food or water. If used correctly, it can be ten times as deadly as a rifle or grenade." Artem feels Yuna's eyes on him. Studying his face, reading the drift of his mind in his vacant stare.

"Show me how to use it," she tells the commissar. He glares at Artem, frowns, then kneels down next to Yuna, instructing her in the finer points of wireless transmission. Artem tries to pay attention—terms like *frequency* and *tuning* and *squelch* come and go—but he is helplessly in thrall to their dizzying height. From their ramshackle perch, he can see all the way to the flat, frozen emptiness that surrounds the dead city. Once, all of Russia looked this way. Then the great cities rose from the earth, Tsaritsyn among them. Eventually

Tsaritsyn became Stalingrad. Now Stalingrad has become something much closer to barren earth than human city. He feels like he's perched at the center of a time machine, giving him a glimpse into humanity's future, when every city has been reduced to ash. *Then,* he thinks, *the animals will reclaim it all.*

"Now!" the commissar says, rising to his feet. "I have given you everything you need to redeem yourselves in the eyes of the motherland. As long as it is light outside, you will be here, in this spot, until darkness falls and you can no longer see. You will keep watch on the Germans below"—he indicates the complex web of rat runs and trenches and fortified strongpoints that make up the Sixth Army's positions—"and radio their movements to the rocket batteries behind the factories. When our katyushas begin to hit their targets, I will know that you are doing your duty."

The commissar takes two steps back, careful not to put his foot through a hole. He produces a silver camera from his pack and raises it to his eye, aiming at Artem and Yuna.

"Try to look like you're glad to be fighting for the motherland," he says. Artem glances at Yuna, who looks both grim and fierce as she stares back at the commissar. "Now, look out over the German positions and point to something in the distance."

The camera clicks and clicks. At last, satisfied with his photographs, the commissar puts the camera away.

"You will be in the next issue of *Red Star,*" the commissar says. "The children who volunteered to be artillery spotters."

Volunteered? Artem thinks. The commissar seems lost in the story he's about to write. He stares beyond them at some imaginary newspaper, moving his hand slowly across the page. "Children of Stalingrad, making the ultimate sacrifice for the motherland."

Artem's heart pounds. *Ultimate sacrifice?*

The commissar begins to climb down the handholds of shell holes in the cement that brought them to this place. "Oh, and try to keep out of sight while you work," he says. "The Germans hate artillery spotters as much as they hate snipers."

CHAPTER

Artem tilts his head against an onslaught of shrieking wind atop the factory. The exposed room offers no protection from the winter that has come down on Stalingrad like the *gamayun* bird-woman who brings the storms with her from the east. The cold blasts through the furry earflaps of his hat, whipping his raw skin. Ice crystals mingle with ash and swirl like tiny bugs, stinging his face.

"Remember how hot it was when we were digging back in August?" Artem says. Yuna is almost entirely hidden inside the greatcoat she scavenged from a dead soldier. She is a gray-green lump at his side, peering carefully around the collapsed wall, down onto the wasteland below. The afternoon is quiet except for the chatter of machine guns over at the Barrikady factory.

"I remember you asking me dumb questions instead of working, like you are now," she says.

Artem raises a field periscope to his eyes. The scope was a gift from Krymov, who told Artem he found it "lying around." Artem believes that's a nice way of saying "I took it from a dead artillery spotter."

The scope is like a miniature version of a submarine's periscope, designed like vertical binoculars that allow you to see over walls. A German sniper looking to kill him will only be able to shoot the top of the scope and not Artem's head.

He sweeps the periscope slowly along the front lines beyond the tractor works. His mind ticks through the ruins. *Repair shop, workers' hut, train yard, rat run, wires—*

"Wires!" he says, pausing the scope. Snaking away from the twisted metal of three bombed-out Panzer tanks are a series of thin black lines—the telltale sign of a communications hub for the German command.

A prime target.

Yuna bends to the American radio. "Where?"

Artem describes the location as best he can. Almost a week of artillery spotting has made him adept at judging distances from his perch atop the factory. "Two kilometers northeast from the edge of the factory."

Artem hears a burst of static, then Yuna's clear, calm voice as she radios the target coordinates.

The screaming comes a moment later. Katyusha rockets, drowning out the wind with their own banshee howls. Fired from launch units attached to trucks, the rockets arc above the factory to the right of Artem and Yuna's position. They duck down and shield their heads with their arms—an air-raid reflex. The rockets are deafening. There is no other sound but their fury, as if they're ripping open the air itself. The explosions are staggered as each rocket strikes the target. The ripple of devastation is drawn out as more pour in.

Artem's eyes are shut. He rests his forehead against a slab of cement. The factory trembles as the rockets hammer the communications post. He feels himself enter a sort of trance. There is a direct line that can be traced from his description of the target to Yuna's fingers on the radio to the soldiers manning the rocket launchers to the Germans in their post, who have surely been obliterated by now. He tells himself that the very Germans whose deaths he just ordered over the wireless radio could have killed Vasily, or soldiers like Chef and Krymov back in their basement. As the noise from the rocket attack dies away, he decides that what he feels most of all is cold.

Eventually, he lifts his head. Yuna gives him a look. He picks up the field periscope and leans into the rubber-ringed eyepiece. Gradually, he lifts his head so that the scope's lens peeks above the remains of the demolished wall.

The aftermath of the rocket attack is easy to spot. He trains the scope on the smoldering wreckage spewing smoke. The frozen earth is blackened and scorched. Bits and pieces of Panzer tanks are strewn about—metal that was once fashioned into armor twisted into new forms. Other than that, there isn't much left of the post. Or the German soldiers who operated it.

"I'd say we got them," Artem says. Next to him, Yuna makes a note on a small pad.

The machine guns in the distance go quiet. There's a brief lull in the symphony of Stalingrad: no guns, no cries, no bombers, no shells. Artem draws cold air in through his nose and takes a few calming breaths.

Suddenly, the scope goes dark. At the same time, a violent tugging wrenches the instrument from his hands. Artem is spun to the right as if by a fierce gust of wind. A dull, bone-rattling pain shoots down his arms. He is aware of shattered glass as the lens and the mirrors inside the scope disintegrate around him. The world turns upside down and he is tossed onto his side. He senses danger all around, without knowing exactly what's happened. A voice in the back of his mind screams: *RUN*.

He scrambles halfway to his feet before he is shoved down hard. His chin connects with an iron girder. Stars pop like cloudburst flak behind his eyes. He tastes blood.

"Sniper!" Yuna hisses in his ear. "Stay down!"

It takes Artem a moment to bring order to the chaos in his mind. They called in the rocket strike. When he moved his periscope above the collapsed wall to survey the scene, a German sniper had caught the movement, lined the scope up in his crosshairs, and blown it away. The force of the shot had numbed his arms and spun him around.

If it wasn't for Yuna's quick thinking, he would have popped his head right back up and made himself a perfect target.

He glances at the shattered pieces of the scope and shudders.

"Where is he?" Artem wonders out loud. "We're up so high."

"We'll have to keep our heads down until it gets dark," Yuna says.

Artem tries to get comfortable. Lying perfectly flat, he stares up at the sky. The sun is nowhere to be found. He tries to recall the last time he felt its warmth on his face. Clouds pass overhead, threading layers of smoke. Somewhere above all that poisoned air, the sky is blue and the sun is shining. He thinks of the cranes.

"Hey, Yuna," he says. "Thanks."

It takes her a while to respond. When she does, her voice is oddly halting. "We made it this far together," she says. "When the Germans captured me, you came and got me. You didn't have to." She laughs. "It was actually really stupid. But you did it." She pauses. "I know this is going to sound strange, but I keep thinking we made it this far because we're together. I don't want to try to get through this by myself."

"I don't, either," Artem says.

Despite the gathering dark and the swirling winds and the sniper's rifle pointed at their perch, he starts to feel a little bit warmer.

CHAPTER

Please, comrade commissar," Artem says. He and Yuna are standing at the foot of the ladder that will take them to the second floor of the factory office, where they can climb up increasingly narrow ledges of exposed iron until they reach their perch. "There's a German sniper who knows we're up there. He'll be waiting for us. We can't go back."

The commissar loads a roll of film into his camera and snaps the compartment shut. He looks at Artem as if he doesn't understand a word he just said.

"*Can't?* What do you mean?"

"He means the sniper will kill us," Yuna says.

"Do you think that when General Chuikov orders an attack, his men tell him they *can't* do it?"

"You're not General Chuikov," Artem blurts out before he can stop himself. The commissar blinks, frowning. A coldness moves across his face. He stares into Artem's eyes. Artem feels like he's back in the sniper's crosshairs.

The commissar moves quickly, with the grace of a striking snake. Clutching his camera in one hand, he takes Artem by the throat with the other. Artem tries to wriggle away to relieve the pressure on his windpipe, but the commissar slams him back against the rungs of the ladder and tightens his grip.

"Do you want me to say it out loud? Very well, boy. You are worth more to the motherland dead than alive. Alive, you are simply a story in *Red Star.* Another tale of heroism in battle. We have plenty of those. But dead? You are a martyr. A rallying cry for our men besieged in these factories. Soldiers so hungry or wounded they can barely move will fight on long past the point of reason to avenge the deaths of the two brave young artillery spotters who sacrificed themselves for Russia. You understand?"

Artem's vision goes fuzzy. He claws weakly at the commissar's hand. Yuna's voice is a distant shout. She tugs at the man's arm to no avail. His mouth curves into a pitiless smile. "Now get up there and do your duty."

He releases Artem's throat. Artem falls to his knees, gasping for air. Yuna glares up at the commissar. "People only fight for you because they're afraid."

He laughs. "I don't care why they fight. As long as there are more dead Germans than dead Russians at the end of it all."

The commissar lets his camera dangle from its strap and draws his pistol. "Now, pull yourself together and climb that ladder. You have until the count of three."

Yuna helps Artem to his feet. He tries to draw a full breath into his burning lungs and doubles over, coughing.

The commissar aims his pistol at Artem. "One."

Artem forces himself to straighten up. His blurred vision makes three overlapping commissars who waver back and forth. The shadows of the ruined factory seem to spread like poured oil. He picks out movement in the haze, figures coming out of the smoke.

The commissar's finger curls over the trigger. "Two."

The figures are all around now. Artem thinks they must be the ghosts of Stalingrad, the voices he hears from the basement shelter.

The commissar looks irritated at what Artem and Yuna are forcing him to do. His mouth begins to form *three.*

A shot rings out: the crack of a rifle.

The commissar falls. Splayed in the dirt, he lies perfectly still, the pistol still clutched in his hand.

The ghosts come forward out of the shadows. The one in front lowers his rifle. Wisps of white smoke curl up from the barrel.

Artem finds his voice. "Vasily?"

CHAPTER

The young man standing before Artem is not a ghost, but neither is he Artem's brother—at least, not the brother he remembers. This frontoviki who comes from the shadows bears a passing resemblance to the boy Vasily used to be—the shock of hair swooping down across his forehead, sticking out from his winter hat. The thick-featured face that appears to be molded from putty. The slightly bent nose. Other than that, he is a stranger. This young man is lean, not stocky, and the kindness in his once-bright eyes has turned to murky, dull gray. There is something else there, too, something that chills Artem to the bone: the way his eyes look right through Artem into a place only Vasily can see.

Vasily steps over the body of the commissar without sparing the corpse a glance. Artem looks around frantically—his brother has just executed General Chuikov's political officer! The Red Army won't think twice about having Vasily shot for such a crime. Yet he appears unconcerned, as do the seven men who stepped out of the shadows with him.

Artem rushes forward and throws his arms around his brother. He can feel Vasily's wiry muscles beneath the greatcoat. Vasily stands there, rifle dangling loosely in his grip, while Artem hugs him. Artem feels an eerie coldness from Vasily that has nothing to do with the weather.

Artem steps back. He glances from side to side, expecting Vasily to say something—anything at all!—and then lead his men away from this place, from the evidence of what he has done. Yet Vasily simply stands there, pinning Artem in that vacant gaze.

Artem swallows. "I did it, Vasily. What you asked me to do. I got Mom across the river. She's alive."

"Good," Vasily says after a while. "That's good." His voice is even and blank. The men at his back stand around casually as if there is no hurry to be anywhere. Artem feels like he's dreaming. Shouldn't they be weeping tears of joy, rushing to fill each other in on the events of their lives?

"This is Yuna," he says.

Vasily's gaze slides languidly to the girl.

"When I heard the Fifty-First was here," Artem says, "and the Germans were attacking with everything they had, I didn't know if you . . ." Artem trails off. "I was scared. But you're alive!"

Vasily doesn't move. He doesn't speak.

"Oh!" Artem says. "I almost forgot. Misha's alive, too! I've got him here, in a basement. He's okay, but he's skinny. Like you. You lost so much weight! Have you been eating horsemeat? We have. It's tough and stringy at first but you get used to it."

Snot is frozen beneath Vasily's nostrils. He makes no attempt to wipe it away.

"Vasily, it's me! It's Artem!"

"You shouldn't be here," Vasily says at last. "You have to leave this place."

"What? No." Artem stands up as straight as he can. "I'm not going anywhere. What's wrong with you?"

German shells pound the factory's southern edge. The ground shakes. Katyushas answer with a shriek. Vasily stares off into the distance.

Artem raises his voice. "Vasily!" He's more terrified now than when they were pinned down by the sniper, or when the commissar was choking him. "Didn't you miss me?"

"No," Vasily says.

Artem's eyes fill with tears. "Don't you love me?"

"No."

He is crying now, weeping openly in front of Yuna and all these soldiers. "Why are you being like this?"

Vasily takes his rifle in two hands and turns to lead his men away. "Forget about me," he says, walking off in the direction of the shelling. The other seven men follow silently.

"Wait!" Artem yells after him. Yuna takes his arm and he brushes her aside. "You can't go! Come with us!"

"Artem," Yuna says, "we can't stay here."

Artem watches as Vasily and the other men melt into the shadows of the factory. He turns to Yuna. "That wasn't Vasily! I mean, it *was,* but that's not how he is, I swear! Something's wrong."

Pure distress sends him into Yuna's arms. Before he knows it, he's crying on her shoulder, letting out the pain and the fear and the horror.

"It's okay," she whispers. "It's going to be okay."

Unlike his brother, Yuna hugs him back.

CHAPTER

The basement is empty except for Krymov sitting in the corner with his leg out straight, propped on a pile of bricks with a thin blanket folded over the top. A bloody bandage is wrapped around his thigh. Misha is curled up in his lap.

"What happened to you?" Artem says, rubbing his hands together, shaking off the chill. Yuna comes in behind him.

"A souvenir from the fascists. Shrapnel."

"Does it hurt?"

"It's nothing." He studies Artem. "But what happened to *you*? You look like you've seen a ghost." He lifts Misha from his lap and hands him to Artem, who cradles the cat in his arms.

"I saw my brother, out there in the factory."

Krymov raises an eyebrow.

"It was all wrong," Artem says, swallowing the lump in his throat.

"He wasn't himself. He wasn't *anybody*. He didn't care about anything."

Yuna comes over with a bit of pork for Misha. The cat nibbles from her hand.

"You can't take it personally," Krymov says. "Fighting here, we have all done terrible things. Things we never knew we were capable of. Things we can't forget."

Artem stops short of telling Krymov that his brother shot the commissar. "He said he didn't miss me. That he didn't love me."

"It's hard to remember what love is in this place," Krymov says gently.

Artem holds Misha tight as Yuna gives him another piece of pork. "Will he ever be the way he was again?"

Krymov looks at him for a long time before he answers. "I wish I could say I knew the answer to that, Artem Romanovich."

Artem glances at the filthy blanket over the entrance to the basement. He imagines running up the stairs, chasing his brother through the dark and dead places of Stalingrad, hounding him until he slips back into the Vasily he used to be. The Vasily who lifted him up that day in Lenin Square. Who showed him the civil war trenches cut into the hills of the Mamayev Kurgan. Who taught him how to catch sturgeon in the Volga.

Outside, the shelling creeps closer. A nearby explosion topples some forlorn structure, and the collapse of iron is deafening. Machine guns open up. Flak bursts in dull pops as Stukas dive for the Red October factory.

Vasily's words run through his head. *You have to leave this place.*

And go where? he asks his brother silently. He thinks of his mother across the river. The half-frozen Volga with its grinding, deadly ice.

"We're getting out of here," he tells Krymov.

Krymov considers this. "What about our friend, the commissar? The one who's going to make us into international superstars?"

"Um," Artem says.

"He dismissed us," Yuna says quickly. "He said we could go."

Krymov considers this. "One can't argue with the wisdom of a commissar. I think I speak for all the men of this illustrious basement when I say that we will miss our furry mascot." Artem goes to Krymov so the man can pet Misha one last time. "Do you know about the caves in the cliffs by the riverbank?"

"Where General Chuikov's headquarters used to be," Yuna says.

"No," Krymov says. "North of there. Deeper caves than most people know about. My father took me to explore them when I was younger. You might be safe there, for a while."

Artem glances at Yuna. She nods. He lifts Misha and tucks the cat inside his greatcoat.

"Take care of yourselves," Krymov says.

"You too," Artem says.

Krymov gives them a smart salute, then leans back against the wall and closes his eyes. Artem moves the blanket aside and climbs the stairs. Yuna follows. Smoke stings his eyes when he reaches the top. The great iron ribs of the factory are barely visible. Soldiers slip in and out of the gray-black mist. Artem pauses for a moment, waiting for his brother to come running up to tell him that he's better now, that everything can go back to the way it was. Nothing happens. Yuna takes his arm and they turn away from the factory.

CHAPTER

DECEMBER

"Artem! Wake up!"

He opens his eyes. "I'm already awake."

"Your eyes were closed."

"I was *trying* to sleep."

He sits up. Yuna's face is drained of color in the light that leaks in through the mouth of the cave. Next to her, faint orange embers smolder. Scattered next to the firepit are the tiny bones of their dinner: a pair of rats that Misha caught. Snuggled against his leg underneath a rancid blanket, the cat stirs, meows once, and goes back to sleep.

"Come see this!"

Artem groans and shivers. His breath comes out in puffs of white. "Do I have to?"

Without another word, Yuna takes his arm and pulls him up to his feet. The blanket falls away. He watches with envy as Misha curls up. "You're always grabbing my arm."

Yuna leads him to the edge of the cave. After living here for more than two weeks, Artem has come to think of it as home. It's not bad, as Stalingrad shelters go: a deep gouge in a cliff overlooking the river. Other than a few stragglers looking to trade what little they have for food, no one bothers them.

Of course, Artem knows the real reason they are mostly left alone is because the army is using the nearby caves to store frozen bodies until they can be carried across the river. But he doesn't like to dwell on that.

At the cave's opening, Artem shields his eyes. Compared to the darkness inside, even the dreary gray morning is bright on the icy river.

"You see?" Yuna says excitedly.

It takes Artem a moment to realize what's happening as he looks down upon a hive of activity. The Volga is positively bustling. Trucks tow massive howitzers with barrels the size of tree trunks. Sleds piled high with crates of ammunition carve tracks in the snow. Entire divisions of men march in formation past barges stuck fast in the ice. There are ambulances, nurses, engineers, *food*.

All of it comes from landings across the river, and all of it is headed their way. Toward Stalingrad.

"The river's frozen," Artem says. "They're crossing." He looks at Yuna. "They're crossing!"

She laughs. "They're crossing," she agrees. "Which means—"

"*We* can cross." He rushes back inside the cave. Yuna follows.

"Should we wait till it gets dark?"

He tosses her the blanket. Misha stretches and glares up at him. "We're going right now. Unless you want to eat another rat."

"Okay. Just give me a few minutes to pack my stuff."

Artem bursts out laughing. Their possessions consist of the ragged clothes they're wearing, a very skinny cat, a filthy blanket, and some ever-present lice. He takes Misha in his arms. Yuna wears the blanket like a shawl.

A few minutes later they stand together at the river's edge. Soldiers are already unloading bodies from the caves and stacking them in flatbed trucks for the journey. A sheet of ice stretches as far as they can see to the north and south. Three kilometers to the east, the opposite bank awaits.

"'Not one step back,'" Artem mutters.

"You think anyone will try to stop us?"

Artem points at the howitzers. "Those guns are what we needed to break the stalemate at the factories." A quick flash of Vasily's blank stare pops into his head and he pushes it away. "Now that we can get supplies across the river, the Germans are really done for."

What information about the battle he has picked up comes from those visitors to their cave. Operation Uranus has all but succeeded. Using the city itself as bait, the Red Army has managed to perform a huge encirclement of the German Sixth Army.

It is only a matter of time before the freezing, starving invaders are completely destroyed.

"At this point," he says, "I don't think anybody will care about two kids in dirty rags."

"The commissar would," Yuna points out. "There are still lots of men like him."

Artem takes his first defiant step onto the ice. "I guess we'll find out."

CHAPTER

It takes Artem and Yuna several hours to cross the river. The slick surface of the ice makes for slow going, and they give the huge army convoys a wide berth. The march of troops and supplies from the east bank seems endless. Artem marvels at the size of the guns being pulled across. Soldiers in their white winter uniforms sing "The Little Blue Shawl." Nobody pays them any mind.

As they get closer to the east bank, Artem glances back over his shoulder. He has never seen the city from here. It unfurls in a ragged line of low smoky ruins. He can scarcely believe they survived there for five months. He reaches out and finds Yuna's gloved hand, squeezing it. When he releases it, she tightens her grip and pulls him close. Together, they walk in the shadow of the giant artillery pieces looming over the riverbank.

Artem is dazed by the world they enter as they step off the ice. There is order here. Uniforms are neat. Machinery is in working order. It is an atmosphere of military precision. Incredible how it all becomes chaos as soon as the troops hit the west bank and enter the horrors of Stalingrad.

"Look!" Yuna points at a whitish-gray blur moving along the barren earth, just beyond the gun emplacements. It crests a low ridge and stops.

Artem meets its eyes for a moment. He notes the white stripe up the middle of its pointy head. "Sand badger," he says in a reverent whisper. How long has it been since he's seen anything but rats? *"Meles leucurus."*

He waves at the badger. It stares him down for another second, then scampers over the ridge and disappears. A peaceful feeling blossoms in his chest. He thinks it might be the first small stirrings of relief.

CHAPTER

"We're looking for Anna Olegovna Sokolov."

The nurse at the entrance to the field hospital shrugs. Her uniform is spattered with blood. "Is she a sniper?"

"She's my mother."

"Civilian?"

"Yes."

The nurse points to a wooden structure built from rough-hewn timber, like an enormous mountain cabin. "Try that one."

"We just came from there," Yuna protests.

"They pointed us here," Artem says.

The nurse shrugs again. She mops her brow with a soiled cloth. "There's a war going on, comrade. We can't keep track of everyone." She frowns and glances at the furry lump peeking out from Artem's coat. "Is that a cat?"

"Yes."

"Very nice. Good luck to you."

The nurse turns and vanishes through the doorway. A sour heat coming from inside the field hospital hangs in her wake. Harsh chemical smells mingle with the stench of rot.

Artem and Yuna keep searching. They scan row upon row of wounded soldiers on cots. Some of them reach out, call Artem and Yuna by different names. *The names of their own children,* Artem thinks.

After several days of this, they abandon the hospitals and resort to asking anyone who will talk to them about a stocky woman with a broken leg who arrived in October.

"You mean the mechanic," says a man peeling potatoes and tossing them into a huge metal pot.

"I don't think so," Artem says.

The man smirks. "If you hang around by the truck depot, you'll find her."

Artem and Yuna head for a flat expanse full of Russian trucks and American-made jeeps. They move down rows of vehicles like they're once again searching hospital cots. Soldiers and workers mill about. Engines ignite, cough, sputter, die. Disassembled tank parts are strewn for what seems like several kilometers.

Suddenly, Yuna grabs his arm. "Look!"

She points to a pair of legs sticking out from beneath the front of a truck. One leg is clad in grease-spattered trousers. The other is in a cast. Artem walks over with his heart in his throat. As he approaches, he can hear the clanking of metal tools and cursing.

"Mom?"

The clanking ceases. The figure beneath the truck slides out on a wooden board attached to four wheels.

Anna Olegovna Sokolov stares up at them. A wrench falls from her hand. She bolts upright on the board. "Artem." She says his name quietly, like she can't believe what she's seeing and must convince herself. "Is it really you?"

Misha's head pops out of his greatcoat. His mother laughs. A moment later, all three of them are wrapped in an embrace.

"I never gave up hope," she says. Artem and Yuna sit with her, heedless of the frozen ground and the failing light. Artem fills her in on everything: the oberst, the canteens, the hand grenade, the rescue at the German strongpoint, the factories, the commissar—even Natasha.

"What will happen to her?" Yuna asks.

A bitterness comes over Anna Olegovna. "She made her choice, this Natasha. She wanted to be German so badly. Now she will die with them."

Artem resumes his story and only begins to falter when it comes to Vasily. He finds that he can't put into words the person his brother has become.

But Anna Olegovna doesn't seem as horrified as Artem was. "Whatever he needs to do to survive," she says. "If he needs to become someone else for a while, at least he is still among the living."

They fall silent. Nobody wants to state the obvious: that it has been more than two weeks since he saw his brother at the tractor works. Two weeks of fierce fighting. Two weeks of encircled Germans waging a desperate battle to stave off their inevitable defeat. Who knows what has happened to his brother in that time.

Artem doesn't mention the conversation he had with Krymov. That even if Vasily survives, there's no telling if he will return to the boy he was.

Yuna clears her throat. "Anna Olegovna," she says, "I wanted to thank you. Without you and Artem, I would be—"

"Nonsense," Artem's mother interrupts. "Without *you*, we wouldn't be here together. Besides, I always wanted a daughter."

She does not say this with any kind of twinkle in her eye. Artem realizes she is completely serious. Yuna glances at Artem and turns away with a small, bashful smile. He sets Misha on the ground and scratches underneath the cat's chin.

"You hear that, Misha? I have a sister."

Night falls. Artem and Yuna try to help his mother with her crutches, but she waves them off. She takes them inside a concrete workers' hut where she has a corner with a cot all to herself. It is crowded and warm. There are bowls of hearty solyanka and clean water and hot tea.

Artem's mother raps her knuckles on her cast. "Soon this will come off. And the Germans will surrender. After that, we will have more hard choices to make."

"We have to find Vasily," Artem says.

"Yes," his mother agrees. "But after that. There is still the question of where we will go. We must think of your future." She looks from Artem to Yuna. "Both of you."

Artem wonders if he, too, is like Vasily. If the great ruin of Stalingrad has worked its dark magic on his own character, turning him into someone else entirely. How would he ever know?

"I think it might help Vasily if there's a home for him to come back to," Artem says carefully.

His mother looks surprised. "You mean Stalingrad? You want to *stay*?"

"Will people rebuild it?" Yuna asks.

"Yes," Artem's mother says. "I suppose they will. But it will take years. Your entire childhoods, perhaps."

"Then I want to help," Artem says. "For Vasily." *Whether he's alive or dead*, he thinks. *Or somewhere in between.* "And for the animals."

"Me too," Yuna says.

"Your father would be proud," Artem's mother says. They sip tea and talk in whispers long into the night.

Eventually, Artem closes his eyes and listens to his mother and Yuna fall asleep. He drifts off for an hour or two but wakes again just before dawn. He rises from his blanket, puts on his greatcoat, and gives Misha a soft pat on the head. Then he slips out alone into the frigid morning.

He sits on a bench outside the workers' hut, listening to the never-ending business of war behind the front lines bustle all around him. As the light of another gray day crawls across the sky, Artem watches a flock of partridges soar out over the river.

Winter birds, he thinks. Birds that don't migrate, even when it's freezing.

Birds that stay no matter what.

AUTHOR'S NOTE

One commonly quoted fact about the battle of Stalingrad is that the average life expectancy of a Red Army soldier was twenty-four hours. I'm not sure if this is true, exactly—or if it's even possible to determine—but it's probably not too far off.

Other statistics from the battle—one million soldiers and civilians killed, one million more wounded or captured—are so overwhelming as to be almost incomprehensible. But as I was writing this book, there was something about the notion of twenty-four hours that haunted me. The thought of a young soldier being ferried across the Volga, knowing in his heart that he has perhaps one more day to live, seemed to evoke both colossal waste of life on a grand scale and the threads of everyday heroism woven into the greatest tragedies. In this book I've attempted to pull those threads with respect, authenticity, and an appreciation for the sacrifices of the Red Army soldiers and the citizens of Stalingrad.

To that end, the work of Vasily Grossman was an essential resource. Grossman was a Soviet journalist who spent many months in Stalingrad, living among the soldiers and reporting on life and death in the besieged city. It is through his eyes that I discovered incredible details like the Russian stove dug into the earth, which made it into this book. I recommend both his epic novel, *Life and Fate*, and his reporting from Stalingrad and beyond collected in *A Writer at War*, edited and translated by Antony Beevor and Luba Vinogradova.

I have to cite Antony Beevor a second time for *Stalingrad: The Fateful Siege: 1942–1943*. This book examines the massive scope of the battle from the beginning of Operation Barbarossa and the German army's initial advance into the Soviet Union to their eventual encirclement and destruction at Stalingrad. It's full of vital information about troop movements and the details of warfare, along with character sketches and quotes from observers and participants. It is from this book that I learned that more than 10,000 civilians survived the entire battle in the ruins of the city—a fact that Beevor calls "the most astonishing part of the whole Stalingrad story."

Jochen Hellbeck's *Stalingrad: The City That Defeated the Third Reich* functions as an oral history, containing the first-person impressions of soldiers, officers, nurses, and other participants on both the Soviet and German sides. Here I found many details regarding urban battle tactics and the role and behavior of political officers that I never would have discovered otherwise.

Finally, David L. Robbins' novel *War of the Rats* provided valuable insight into sniper tactics and Red Army culture, wrapped up in the fascinating story of the famous Russian sniper Vasily Zaitsev. He's the guy played by Jude Law in the movie *Enemy at the Gates,* which is based on Robbins' book.

Like I said when we last crossed paths back in East Berlin—and Chernobyl before that—without the authors and works mentioned above, this book would not exist. Any historical inaccuracies, geographical impossibilities, and tweaks to time and space should be blamed on me and me alone.

Thanks for reading. See you next time.

ABOUT THE AUTHOR

Andy Marino is the author of *Escape from Chernobyl*, *Escape from East Berlin*, and several other novels for young readers. He lives in upstate New York with his wife and two dogs. You can visit him at andy-marino.com.